Teddy Jo
and the
Wild Dog

Teddy Jo

and the
wild
dog

HILDA STAHL

WindRider BOOKS
Tyndale House Publishers, Inc., Wheaton, Illinois

Second printing, December 1987

Library of Congress Catalog Card Number 83-71016
ISBN 0-8423-6948-1, paper
Copyright © 1983 by Hilda Stahl
Printed in the United States of America

Dedicated with love to
Joan Naomi Bradfield

contents

1

The Hike

Teddy Jo carefully laid her spoon next to her empty cereal bowl and looked across the table at Paul. He was taking his last bite of Cheerios. She glanced quickly at Mom and Dad, then back to Paul and motioned with her eyes that it was time. He scraped back his chair, suddenly afraid that Dad was in one of his new moods, the one where he wanted to spend more time with them. Today was not the day. He and Teddy Jo were going on a hike.

Teddy Jo could almost read her little brother's mind as they walked toward the back door. Paul's shoelace clicked on the linoleum and Teddy Jo frowned. Paul was eight years old. Would she have to tie his shoelaces for the rest of his life? When he was as old as Grandpa, would she have to follow him around just to see that his shoes were tied?

"Wait a minute, Teddy Jo," said Mom as she

set down her steaming cup of coffee. She still had on her fluffy pink robe.

Teddy Jo's heart sank and she turned around, her blue eyes watchful.

"You can't leave the house without brushing your hair." Mom shook her head. She and Paul had the same dark brown hair and blue eyes.

Teddy Jo made a face, then rushed to the bathroom only to find that Linda was inside with the door locked.

"I just got in here," snapped Linda from inside where she was carefully examining her face for blemishes.

"My brush is in there and I have to brush my hair right now." Teddy Jo rubbed her hands down her jeans and twisted the toe of her hiking shoes in the soft carpet.

The door opened and Linda thrust out the brush, then slammed and locked the door again. Teddy Jo ran to her yellow and white bedroom and quickly brushed the tangles from her dark hair. She clipped in two barrettes to hold it out of her slender face, then dashed back to find Paul. He was trying to look invisible, his pale face turned toward the door, his thin body tense.

"Where are you two going?" asked Larry with a dark brow cocked.

Teddy Jo shot a look at Paul, then turned to Dad. "For a hike. And then to check on the animals at Grandpa's."

Larry rubbed his cheek and his whiskers rasped. "Just see that you're home before dark."

Teddy Jo almost let out a breath of relief, then managed a smile. "We will be." She didn't want Dad trailing along with them, but she didn't want to hurt his feelings if he asked if he could go with them.

Paul rushed out with Teddy Jo into the cool October morning, zipping his jacket as he ran across the damp grass to the sidewalk. Maybe today they'd see the wild dog again. Maybe today they'd find her pups. His stomach fluttered and he shivered as he looked at Teddy Jo.

"Maybe today, Paul," she whispered, her blue eyes sparkling with excitement at the thought of seeing the wild dog. If they found the pups and took them to Grandpa's maybe Mom and Dad would give in and let them have a dog of their own. Who could resist the cute tan and white puppies? She pushed her hands into her jacket pockets, then smiled at Paul. A car drove past and they crossed the street, then walked quickly toward the woods just outside of Middle Lake.

"I sure was scared that Dad would come with us," said Paul, shaking his head. The cool wind turned the tip of his small nose pink.

"It's funny that he wants to do things with us. He never bothered with us before." Teddy Jo walked around a sandbur patch. "I think he's beginning to want a real family just like Grandpa said."

"He wants to take me rabbit hunting after school sometime." Paul wrinkled his forehead and shook his head. "I don't want to shoot a rabbit. What if we shoot one that Grandpa nursed back to health?"

"Dad thinks it's dumb for Grandpa to take care of sick and hurt animals. But I don't! I want to help Grandpa always!" How would it be at Grandpa's now since he and Anna Sloan had married? When they got back from their honeymoon, would everything be different? She remembered the summer she was ten and she'd stayed with Grandpa and learned to love him and love Jesus. Now she had to share him with one more person and that person was her new grandma.

"Do you think Anna Sloan will be a nice grandma?"

Teddy Jo stopped and looked down at Paul in surprise. Sometimes she wondered if he could read her mind. "We'll have to wait and see."

But would they really? In the past year that Grandpa and Anna had been seeing each other, Grandpa hadn't had as much time for them. It would probably continue to be that way. Teddy Jo sighed and looked down at the brown weeds, then up at the tall trees, many already bare for the winter. Others were bright yellows and oranges and reds. If Grandpa were with them right now he'd be telling them just which trees were what. And he'd be helping them look for the wild dog and her pups.

Teddy Jo walked toward the bright red sumac that Grandpa said was deer food. Maybe the wild dog had hidden her pups in the middle of the shrubs. Shivers ran up and down her back just thinking of it.

Paul leaned down and watched a tan and black woolly bear crawl across a wide leaf. He held his hand down and the fuzzy caterpillar crawled onto his hand. He grinned and looked quickly toward Teddy Jo. She probably didn't want him to waste time petting a woolly bear when he was supposed to be looking for the wild dog. Quickly he dropped the hairy creature and ran after Teddy Jo. Suddenly she stopped, her head up, her eyes wide, and Paul ran right into her with a thud. She grabbed his thin arm.

"Shhh! I heard something," she whispered, her palms wet with nervous perspiration. Today she just had to find the dog! School hadn't been all that great and Grandpa was gone on his honeymoon and Dad was acting very strange. Something had to be good about today, and finding the pups would be the very best.

Paul heard a noise too and he waited beside Teddy Jo, nervously fingering the zipper pull tab at the neck of his jacket. His stained

13

brown jacket felt too hot and too tight. His grass-stained blue jeans sagged at his thin hips and would have fallen off if his belt were looser.

Teddy Jo started to take another step, then froze as she saw another movement.

Just then a tall boy with shaggy brown hair jumped around the sumac, a .22 in his hands. "Got ya! Don't take another step!"

Paul huddled closer to Teddy Jo. She lifted her chin and her eyes flashed with anger.

"Roger Peck, how dare you point that gun at us! That's not a toy! I'll tell my dad on you and he'll make sure you never take my sister out again!" Teddy Jo's voice rose. The last angry word stuck in her throat.

Roger Peck's face turned a dull red and he lowered the gun. "You sure can't take a joke, can you?"

"That was not a joke! What're you doing out here with that gun?" Teddy Jo pointed at the gun and scowled. She hated for people to hunt and kill the wild animals around her. What if Roger saw the wild dog and killed it? A bitter taste filled her mouth and she wanted to leap on Roger and grab the .22 away from him. How could Linda like such a dumb boy?

"You think you're real smart, don't you, Teddy Jo Miller?" Roger took a step toward her and she shrank back, Paul pressing close to her side. "Well, you won't have to worry about me hanging around anymore. Me and my dad are leaving."

"I'm glad," said Teddy Jo loudly and firmly and Paul echoed it in a whisper.

Roger turned away, then stopped. "There's that dumb dog again." He raised his gun and Paul screamed and Teddy Jo lunged at Roger, knocking the barrel of the gun into the air. The crack of the shot was loud in her ear. For one wild minute she thought he'd hit his target, but the large collie ran into the woods.

Roger clicked on the safety and glared at Teddy Jo. "Don't you ever do such a dumb thing again! I could've hurt you or even shot you!"

Rage turned Teddy Jo's face red and she doubled her fists at her sides. "Don't you ever try to shoot that dog! She has pups."

Roger shrugged. "Why should I care?"

Paul bit his tongue to keep from saying something really mean. He wanted to kick Roger Peck right in the leg, but he stood beside Teddy Jo and let her do all the talking. She was good at that. And if she really wanted to, she could beat Roger to a pulp. She was small for a twelve year old, but she was tough.

"I'm glad you're moving," said Teddy Jo, barely able to stand still. Once she would've torn him to shreds, but since she'd become a Christian she had determined to be like Jesus. And Jesus sure didn't go around beating up people.

Roger started to speak, then snapped his

mouth closed and strode away, his .22 on his shoulder, his head high.

Teddy Jo clamped her hand on Paul's thin shoulder and looked toward the woods where they'd seen the wild dog. Large tears of disappointment filled her eyes, then slowly slipped down her hot cheeks. Now the wild dog would be scared off.

2
Smokey

Teddy Jo pulled off her tan jacket and tied the sleeves around her narrow waist. She lifted her dark hair off her neck and let the cool breeze dry the perspiration. This Saturday had to be better than last when Roger Peck had shot at the wild dog and scared it off. This Saturday she and Paul had to find the pups.

"Don't look so sad, Teddy Jo." Paul touched her bare arm, then pushed his hands deep into his loose jeans pockets. The back of his hair stood on end from sleeping on it, then not brushing it with water the way Grandpa had showed him to do. "We prayed that we'd see the pups today. We'll see them!"

Teddy Jo smiled. Paul sounded so sure of himself that it did make her feel better. "We'll find them and then we'll take them to Grandpa's. Maybe they'll be tame by the time he gets home next week."

"Then Dad will see them and let us keep them." Paul danced around a thorny bush and his blue eyes sparkled. "I'll let mine sleep right on my bed."

Teddy Jo grinned as they walked from state property to Peck's land. Roger hadn't been in school all week and Linda had been moping around because she missed him a lot. "With Roger Peck gone, we should for sure find the dog and the puppies. I just bet Dad will let us have one." Her stomach tightened and the smile left her face. Dad was sure a lot nicer than he had been, but he wasn't nice enough yet to let them have a dog. He said that dogs belonged in the country. He said that someone else could pay out good money for dog food and shots and a license.

"I'll think up a great name for my dog and he'll come any time I call him." Paul stopped in the clearing and looked toward the deserted house and shed. Maybe the wild dog had hid her pups there since the Pecks had moved away.

Teddy Jo wrinkled her small nose. Once they'd lived in worse looking places than this run-down farmhouse, but not any longer. Grandpa had sold his precious black walnut trees and bought a house in Middle Lake for them. It was the best house she'd ever seen and certainly the best she'd ever lived in. Roger probably never knew what it was like to live in a nice house. Maybe he and his dad had found a nice place in the city like he told Linda he would. At least they were gone from here and he could no longer shoot at the wild dog.

A bird flew from a tree branch and landed on the high wire that led from a tall pole to the house. A strange bumping noise came from inside the old shed and Teddy Jo gripped Paul's arm fearfully.

"Listen!" Her voice croaked and she swallowed hard.

Paul chewed his bottom lip and tried his best not to shiver. "I'm gonna walk right up to that shed and open that door!" But he shrank back. The hairs on the back of his neck stood on end. He wanted to turn and run but he didn't want Teddy Jo to call him a chicken.

Teddy Jo tugged at her sweater neck, then slowly walked toward the sagging wooden door of the shed. Was someone hiding there? Maybe Roger? Or was it a wild animal that would spring on them when she opened the door?

She rubbed her damp palm down her jeans, then slid back the wooden latch and pulled open the door.

A horse nickered weakly. The morning sun streamed inside and fell across the back of a dark horse tied to the side of the shed. His back was swayed and his ribs stuck out. He turned his head as far as the dirty nylon rope would allow and nickered again.

"How awful!"

Paul pushed in to stand in the doorway beside Teddy Jo. "I think that's Roger's horse Smokey."

"Why would he leave him here? It looks like he hasn't had food or water for days!" Anger rushed through her and she clamped her teeth together, wishing with all her might that she could get at Roger Peck.

A mouse scurried across the floor and out of sight behind an empty box. Smokey nickered again, sounding even weaker.

"We have to help him, Teddy Jo! We can't just leave him!" Paul hated the quiver in his voice and he cleared his throat. "I'm going to walk right up to him and lead him out of this terrible shed."

"Wait!" Teddy Jo caught his arm and he was glad that she had. He really wouldn't have walked up to the horse, but he wanted her to think he would. Someday he'd be so brave that he could do anything, even punch Roger Peck.

Slowly Teddy Jo walked alongside the dark horse. "Easy, Smokey. I came to help you." She touched his neck and Smokey flinched but didn't jump away. "We'll take you to Grandpa's and take care of you. We won't let that mean Roger Peck starve you to death!" She pulled the rope and carefully turned Smokey and led him into the bright October sunshine. He snorted and bobbed his head and she almost dropped the rope and ran. She'd never led a horse before. Smokey looked gigantic next to her and she knew if he wanted to he could walk right over her.

"I think he needs a drink." Paul looked around for water but couldn't find an outside spigot. "We could take him to that stream in the woods and then to Grandpa's."

"Good idea, Paul." Sometimes he amazed her. He wasn't as dumb as some of his teachers said.

At the stream Smokey snorted and pushed his nose deep into the water. He drank and drank, not wanting to leave. Teddy Jo jerked on the rope.

"Help me, Paul! Help me get him away from the water!"

Paul hesitated, then grabbed the rope and pulled with Teddy Jo. Finally Smokey turned away from the stream and walked with them down the slightly worn path. Just then a dog barked and Teddy Jo stopped short and stared with wide blue eyes toward the sound.

"It's our dog," whispered Paul, his heart racing faster. "I know it is!"

Teddy Jo nodded. "Maybe if we're real quiet the dog will walk right up to us."

"Maybe."

Smokey bobbed his head and Teddy Jo almost lost her balance. She stepped close to

Smokey and slipped her arm over his neck. "We're waiting for our dog, Smokey. Be patient awhile, then we'll take you to Grandpa's and take good care of you. We'll never let that bad Roger Peck be mean to you again."

A squirrel chattered from the top of a pine tree. The dog barked again, this time closer. Teddy Jo bit her bottom lip and stood very still. Smokey smelled dusty.

Paul stood as still as the trees around him. The dog would probably think he was a strange-shaped bush and walk right up to him. Shivers of excitement ran up and down his spine and he smiled. The dog would think he was a smiling bush or maybe a young smiling tree. He almost laughed out loud at his thoughts, then bit back the laugh. He dare not make even a peep or it would scare the dog away before they saw it.

Finally the big gold collie stepped from the shelter of the trees onto the path several yards away. She reminded Teddy Jo of the picture of Lassie on a coloring book that she'd had when she was nine.

Teddy Jo sucked in her breath. Oh, how she wanted to slip her arms around the wide white ruff of the collie's neck!

The dog lifted her nose, then turned and saw Teddy Jo and Paul. In a flash she ran into the trees and was gone from sight.

Paul raced after the collie but Teddy Jo

called, "Come back, Paul. You'll get lost all by yourself."

Paul hesitated beside a blackberry bush, then finally turned and walked back to the path, his shoulders drooping and his head down. One more disappointment and he might just throw himself on the ground and scream and kick and curse the way Teddy Jo had before she'd become a Christian. "I want to follow her and find her pups, Teddy Jo!"

"Well, you can't. How can we with Smokey?" Teddy Jo tugged on the rope and Smokey walked with her along the path. One of these days they'd see the big collie and they'd follow her right to her puppies, then they'd take the puppies to Grandpa's and feed them and take care of them and make pets out of them.

Teddy Jo muttered the words under her breath with a determined look on her face. She had to have a dog of her own! With Grandpa married and giving all of his time to Anna Sloan, she needed a dog, a real dog that would learn tricks and lick her face and sleep at her feet in her yellow and white bedroom.

With a weary, discouraged sigh she led Smokey toward the pen in back of Grandpa's empty house. It still seemed strange to have Grandpa gone, stranger still to think when he came back he'd no longer live alone. Maybe he'd never call her Teddy Bear Jo again.

Paul held the gate open and Teddy Jo walked inside with Smokey. Just a few weeks ago a young buck had stayed in the pen. Just before the wedding Grandpa had said the whitetail deer was fit and healthy and he'd set him free.

Teddy Jo unhooked the rope from the bridle and Smokey stood in one spot with his head down, his nose almost touching the grass in the pen. He blew out his nose, then slowly snapped off a mouthful of grass.

"I'll get him water," Paul said over his shoulder as he ran to the shed to get a bucket.

Teddy Jo patted Smokey's dusty shoulder. "We're going to get you healthy again, Smokey. Me and Paul will take good care of you. I promise." Not even Roger Peck could stop her. He was gone for good. Wasn't he?

Several minutes later Paul stood at the fence, watching Smokey. "I think Smokey's a good name for him."

"Me, too." Teddy Jo leaned against the gate. "All animals should have names."

Teddy Jo looked down at Paul. "Oh?"

Paul hesitated, then said in a rush, "I named the big gold collie Queen!"

Teddy Jo sucked in her breath. "Queen. Yes. Yes! Queenie is a perfect name for our dog." She closed her eyes and saw herself riding across the field on Smokey with Queen and her puppies running along beside. Her fingers itched to paint the picture she saw in her head.

Paul looked across to where last fall he had helped Grandpa plant black walnut seedlings for his future and wondered if Queen had ever walked this close to Grandpa's place. What if she walked right into the yard with her puppies behind her?

"I thought I'd find you kids here."

Teddy Jo spun around with a gasp. Dad stood there with a smile on his face and a gun in his hands.

3
Hunting with Dad

"You two got away this morning before I could ask if you wanted to go rabbit hunting with me." Larry walked to Teddy Jo's side. "I told your mom that I'd find you and spend some time with you today."

Teddy Jo's heart sank. She sure didn't want to go hunting. Too bad she couldn't disappear and leave Paul alone to go with Dad. She darted a look at Paul and he looked as if he wanted to hide.

"We found a horse," said Paul. He inched away from Dad.

"What a horse!" Larry shook his dark head, then propped the .22 against the fence. "Somebody treated that animal bad!"

"It was Roger Peck!" Teddy Jo clenched her fists. "But luckily we found Smokey before he died and we brought him here." She told Larry the story and he rubbed his cheek and scowled.

"Roger better never show his face around me! I can't understand people who mistreat animals," Larry continued as he walked to Smokey and gently stroked his sunken side.

Teddy Jo shot a surprised look at Paul, then they walked inside the pen while Larry talked about the horse.

"I say if you can't take proper care of an animal, then don't have one. This horse is in a bad way."

"We'll take care of him," said Paul, nodding hard until his hair bounced. "Before long, he'll be strong and healthy and we'll ride him."

"You don't know how to ride a horse." Larry shook his head. "And I don't want you on this animal unless Ed's around to help you. Or I am."

"Grandpa will help us," said Teddy Jo quickly. "He knows everything!"

"Well, yes, I know Ed knows most things." Larry slowly walked out of the pen and Teddy Jo thought he looked sad and alone.

She nudged Paul, then ran after Larry. "Do you know how to ride, Dad?"

"Never had a horse. But I know enough to help you on and off." Larry picked up his .22. "Lock the gate, Paul, and come on. We're going rabbit hunting." He puffed up with pride and Teddy Jo and Paul hung back.

Teddy Jo locked her hands behind her back and tried to think of something to say to get out of going without hurting Dad's feelings, but nothing came to mind. How awful it would be to watch him shoot a rabbit! Why didn't Paul say something or do something? She looked helplessly at him, but he was staring off into space, his face pale and his back stiff. She looked back at Dad and she could see in his face that he knew their hesitation and was hurt by it.

She plucked at the jacket sleeves tied around her waist. Grandpa had said that love always thought of the other person. He had showed her in her Bible in Romans 5:5 that God's love in her heart could be shared with help from the Holy Spirit. She could love as God loved and she could love Dad even though he hadn't loved her or paid attention to her until the past few weeks.

She lifted her chin and smiled brightly. "Paul and I will go hunting with you, Dad."

"But please, God, don't let there be any-thing to shoot!" Teddy Jo prayed.

Paul jerked around and stared at Teddy Jo as if she'd lost her mind. He sure didn't want to go hunting! He wanted to stay right here and watch Smokey. But he couldn't say any-thing. Slowly he walked after Teddy Jo and Dad. He kicked at the grass and stained the toe of his tennis shoe. One of these days he'd tell Dad just what he thought of going hunting.

Several minutes later Larry stopped suddenly and Teddy Jo almost bumped into him. Her mouth went bone-dry as she watched him raise his .22 to his shoulder. His face was intent and watchful, his body poised. He looked short and slight standing in the woods among the trees and not big and tall like Grandpa Korman.

Paul looked at the spot in the underbrush where Dad's gun pointed and he saw the brown furry rabbit sitting under a thorn bush. His stomach tightened and he thought he was going to be sick. Frantically he looked around for a way to scare the rabbit away without Dad knowing that he'd done anything.

Teddy Jo opened her mouth to shout, then snapped it closed. Dad would get mad if she scared away the rabbit.

Larry aimed and fired and the rabbit leaped and bounded away. Larry frowned and Teddy Jo and Paul smiled.

"You aren't supposed to be happy because I missed." Larry ejected the shell with an angry snap. "I must've lost my touch or it's you two kids. I know how you're feeling! I know that you don't want to be with me or see me hunt. But I don't care! You're stuck with me as a dad and we'll make the most of it."

Teddy Jo stared down at the knot of sandburs on her shoestring. Would Dad get so mad that he'd walk out on the family like he'd done once before when she was ten? Oh, that would be terrible! Finally she lifted her blue eyes to his. "Dad, we don't like hunting, but we like being with you. We'll go with you and be glad and we'll try real hard not to feel bad if you shoot a rabbit."

Paul barely shook his head. He sure wasn't glad to go with Dad and he'd feel real bad if Dad shot something. Why couldn't Teddy Jo keep her mouth shut? Then maybe Dad would tell them to get away from him and leave him to hunt alone and in peace.

Larry cleared his throat and shifted from one foot to the other, then strode ahead, his back stiff, his .22 firmly in his hands.

A dog barked in the distance and Teddy Jo froze, barely breathing. Finally she looked at Paul and she saw the fear in his eyes. Dad must not see Queenie! He didn't want stray dogs running around.

Larry looked over his shoulder. "I thought you two were coming with me."

"We are," said Teddy Jo breathlessly. She jerked on Paul's arm and they ran to catch up to Dad. A twig snapped under her foot and she jumped. Maybe if she could manage to snap lots of twigs, she'd scare away Queen and any other animals around.

Larry ducked under a low branch, then held it back for Teddy Jo and Paul. "We've had some bad years, kids, but no longer. We're going to get to know each other and we're going to do things together."

Teddy Jo thought about her artwork and about the blue ribbon she'd won last year for the best drawing of a wild animal in its natural

31

habitat. Dad hadn't been interested in her art then, and he probably wouldn't be now. Sure, he'd looked at the drawing when she'd pushed it under his nose, then he'd said he'd sure like to get a bead on a buck like that. He hadn't said a word about the blue ribbon or the drawing. He probably wouldn't even after she was rich and famous.

She almost tripped over a fallen branch, then caught herself and walked two steps behind Dad and Paul. She dabbed the dampness from her forehead and lifted her long hair off her neck.

Birds flew from tree to tree. Squirrels chattered, then grew quiet.

Finally Larry stopped in a clearing and looked around. He walked to a fallen log and sat down, stretching his legs out in front of him. His hunting shoes looked large and awkward and he smelled of sweat and hot wool.

Paul looked around in alarm, then darted a look at Teddy Jo. This was the spot where they'd last seen Queen and her pups. What if the pups were hidden nearby? What if Dad saw them? His legs gave way and he sank to the log hopelessly.

Teddy Jo licked her dry lips. What if Queen walked right out in front of them now? Would Dad shoot her? She bit back a moan and momentarily closed her eyes. "Dad, can't we go down the hill near the pines?" she asked. She caught Dad's quick look and she knew he'd heard the panic in her voice.

"Just sit down and we'll wait right here. I've hunted rabbits here before and I always get two or three."

Paul locked his hands around his knees and hung on tight.

Teddy Jo slowly sat down, poised and ready to leap up and shout if Queen walked into sight.

Larry crossed his ankles and smiled a pleased smile. "My youngest brother, Tom, and I used to hunt here all the time. We had some fun times before we finally moved away. You kids don't remember Tom, but you would've liked him. He could hunt with the best of 'em and always bring back his limit. I sure would like to see Tom again, but me and him lost touch just like I did with all my brothers."

Teddy Jo forced herself to listen to Dad's story. She'd never heard him talk about his family before. Today was the most words it seemed he'd said to her in all of her twelve years.

Suddenly Larry stopped talking and pulled his feet back and leaned forward, his .22 ready. "Don't make a move," he whispered.

Paul groaned and Teddy Jo wrapped her arms across her thin chest and waited.

Just then a big gold collie stepped out from behind some bushes. It was Queen.

4
Queen

"Whose dog is that?" asked Larry barely above a whisper.

Teddy Jo bit her lip and Paul pulled into himself, looking small and pale and scared.

Larry shot Teddy Jo a sharp look. "Answer me!"

Queen lifted her great head and looked around. She saw them, but didn't run.

"Whose dog?" asked Larry again, this time impatiently.

"Nobody's," whispered Teddy Jo around the hard lump in her throat.

"We can't have strays scaring off deer." Larry pushed off his safety with a click that echoed inside Teddy Jo's head.

"Don't shoot her," said Teddy Jo in a small, tight voice.

"Don't," mouthed Paul. Shivers ran over him and he thought he was going to be sick.

Larry looked down the sights, his finger on the trigger.

Teddy Jo grabbed his arm. "Don't shoot!" Oh, why didn't Queen run away? Why was she standing there?

"Let go of me!" Larry said through clenched teeth. "I won't have a wild dog around."

"Run, Queen!" Paul tried to shout the words, but they came out in a hoarse croak.

Teddy Jo saw Dad's finger move and she bumped against him just as the gun fired and it jerked.

"You crazy girl!" shouted Larry.

"Queenie!" cried Paul.

The big gold collie dropped to the ground, blood flowing from her chest.

"Queenie!" Teddy Jo ran wildly toward the fallen dog.

"Stay away from her!" shouted Larry as he dropped the .22. He ran after Teddy Jo and Paul dashed around him, but Larry caught Paul's arm and jerked him up short. Paul struggled, then gave in and meekly stood beside him. "Theodora Josephine Miller! Don't take another step!"

Teddy Jo froze. She knew Dad meant what he said. Slowly she turned to face him. Bright spots stood out on her cheeks and she trembled. The sun went behind a cloud and a cool breeze blew against her hot body. "You shot Queenie!"

"I didn't kill her," Larry said coldly. "Thanks to you I missed her heart and now I'll have to finish the job to get her out of her misery."

The words pounded in Paul's head and he flung himself against Dad. "You can't kill her! She's got puppies! She's our dog!"

Teddy Jo stamped the groud and doubled her fists. "Don't you dare kill Queen! I'll take her to Grandpa's and fix her up!"

"No!" Larry's voice rang out and he ran to Teddy Jo and caught her before she could reach the collie. "A hurt animal could kill you or tear you apart. It fights when it's in pain. Stay away from that dog! And I mean it, kids. I'll take care of her!"

Teddy Jo shook her head hard. "No, no! You can't kill her! If you do I'll hate you forever and so will Paul and so will Grandpa!" She saw Larry flinch and she knew he'd heard her well.

He shook his head and walked to the dog and stood quietly looking down at her. She lay very still, blood oozing from her and coloring her white and gold hair. "She's going to die if I leave her. I can't let her suffer."

Teddy Jo rushed past and dropped beside Queen. She didn't move even when Teddy Jo touched her head. "She looks dead already!" wailed Teddy Jo, tears filling her eyes as she looked accusingly up at Dad. "You already killed her! I hate you!"

Paul sobbed, then gasped. "Her side moved up and down. She's breathing, Teddy Jo! She's not dead at all!" Relief rushed through him and he dropped beside Teddy Jo and rested his small hand on the dog's side. He felt the heart beat and he bowed his head and let the tears flow freely.

Larry made a strange noise deep in his throat, then roughly pushed Teddy Jo and Paul away from the dog. "If it means that much to you, I'll take the dog to the vet and see what he can do."

"Grandpa would take care of him if he were home," said Teddy Jo, rubbing the tears from her eyes. Oh, why did Grandpa have to be gone now of all times!

"Ed Korman can't do everything," said Larry gruffly. "The bullet is still in the dog. It'll take a vet to get it out." Larry awkwardly picked up the heavy dog. Grandpa could've picked up two dogs that size and never had his legs wobble.

"Teddy Jo, you get my .22 and bring it home. I'll go to the vet's and meet you at home later."

Teddy Jo looked toward Larry and the dog and into the woods where she knew the puppies were. If she told Dad that they wanted to find the puppies, would he let them or would he force them to go home right now? She couldn't take a chance. She impatiently ran to the .22 and picked it up, frowning down at it. How she wanted to toss it away, far away where she wouldn't see it ever again!

At Grandpa's, Larry carefully laid Queen in the back of his battered pickup, then took the .22 from Teddy Jo. "You kids head for home and tell Mom that I'll be there later."

"Will the vet keep Queen?" asked Paul, his blue eyes large in his pale face.

"Probably not, or maybe for a day." Larry strode to the driver's door and jerked it open. "I'll bring Queen here when the vet's done with her. You kids will have your hands full taking care of her and that sway-backed horse too."

"We can do it," said Teddy Jo stiffly. She stood beside Paul and watched gravel fly from under the tires as Dad drove out of the drive onto the dirt road in front of Grandpa's house. Finally she turned to Paul and her heart raced frantically. "We've got to find the puppies or they'll die. We've got to find them now!"

He nodded and sniffed hard. "I'll be right back." He ran to the back door and fumbled with the key they'd hidden under a rock, then disappeared inside.

Teddy Jo knew he'd run to the bathroom and she was glad that he hadn't wet his pants like he sometimes did when he was upset or scared. No way did she want to hunt for the puppies with Paul smelling like a wet bed.

Several minutes later Teddy Jo once again stood in the clearing with Paul beside her. They looked down at the brown patch of blood, then quickly away.

"We'd better stay together, Paul. I sure don't want you to get lost."

"I'm no baby!"

"I know, but we'd better stay together." She looked at the bushel basket that they'd taken from Grandpa's shed. "The puppies should be easy to carry back in this. If you're strong enough."

Paul flexed his muscles. "I sure am strong enough! I'm so strong I bet I could carry that alone." But he knew he couldn't. He was small for his age and he wanted to grow up to be big and strong like Grandpa.

Teddy Jo frowned, but didn't argue with Paul. It never did any good. "We'll have to be very quiet so we can hear them. We'll look first under that tree root where we first saw them with Grandpa."

"I bet they're big now. They were so tiny then and wriggly." Just thinking about them made Paul laugh and his hands itch to hold one.

"They'll have their eyes open by now and maybe will be old enough to eat puppy food and drink milk from a dish." Her heart leaped. She couldn't wait to find the puppies and take them to Grandpa's. Oh, they just had to find them!

Slowly she walked with Paul into the woods to the tree where they'd first seen the puppies. She leaned down, but the hole was empty. Small creatures scurried in the dried leaves and underbrush. A fly buzzed around her head.

"Queenie has to be alive," whispered Paul

with a loud sniff. He rubbed his nose with the
back of his hand. His stomach rumbled and he
shook his head with a frown. This was not the
time to be hungry even if it was past lunchtime.
After they found the puppies he would eat
the sack lunch that he'd left at Grandpa's with
Teddy Jo's.

Teddy Jo tugged the handle she held and
pulled Paul along with her. She stopped, her
head cocked, and listened for a whimpering
sound. The other noises in the woods suddenly
sounded too loud and her heart sank. Well,
she couldn't give up! And she wouldn't!

Later, she stood wearily beside the stream
where they'd watered Smokey. Her legs ached
and she was very hungry. She looked down
at Paul and could see that he was tired too and
his face was smeared with dirt. Hers probably
was too, but it didn't matter. She nudged the
basket sitting at her feet and rubbed her
tired fingers where the wire had cut into them.
Inside the basket lay her jacket and Paul's.

Just then she heard a whimpering noise. Her
head shot up and her blue eyes widened.
It had to be the puppies! She nudged Paul and
put her finger to her lips for silence, then
motioned toward the direction that she'd heard
the sound.

He heard it too and his heart leaped with
excitement. Slowly he walked with Teddy Jo
toward the sound.

There, under a tree, half buried in a hole,

and under leaves were the puppies. Tan and white puppies with black noses and dark eyes. Grandpa had said that they were a cross between collie and German shepherd. Teddy Jo counted four puppies. There had been five. Was one dead or was it hiding?

"One is missing," whispered Paul as he slowly set the basket on the ground.

Teddy Jo knelt beside the puppies. One growled a baby growl at her and she laughed. Slowly, carefully, she picked up a puppy. It was soft and cuddly and she wanted to hug it to her, but she could feel its heart racing in fear. Carefully she laid it on her jacket in the basket.

Paul lifted a puppy and held it against his chest. Nothing had ever felt so good. Finally he laid it in the basket beside the other one.

When the four puppies were in the basket Teddy Jo watched them push against each other, then settle down to sleep. She pushed aside dead leaves and looked for another puppy. She listened for a sound from it, but no sound came. Finally she said, "We'd better go, Paul."

"I guess so," he said, looking around once again.

They lifted the basket, one of them on each side and it was much heavier than before, but the heaviness was a pleasure.

Teddy Jo took three steps, then stopped. "I

have to look again, Paul. It would be terrible to leave a puppy."

Paul stood beside the basket while Teddy Jo walked back to the spot. She dug around once again in the leaves and dirt, then sank back on her legs and looked all around. She saw a movement close to the base of the tree and she leaned forward, every nerve tense.

Slowly she stood, then walked to the spot. What if it were a wild animal that was waiting to bite her? Finally she reached down and carefully moved aside leaves and twigs. A small black nose poked out of a hole and two black eyes looked up at her. It was the missing puppy—and if they'd walked away without him, he'd have died of hunger or been killed by a hungry hawk.

The puppy pushed his nose into her neck and she carried him to the basket, her eyes glowing with happiness. Finally they had the puppies. Maybe soon she and Paul would have a puppy of their own at their own home in Middle Lake.

Paul looked at Teddy Jo and smiled and she knew he was thinking the same thing. Together they picked up the basket and walked toward Grandpa's.

5
Grandpa's Help

Teddy Jo stepped back and smiled with pride. "We did good, Paul. The puppies have a happy home now."

"I sure wish we could take all of them home with us."

"Me, too." Teddy Jo shook out her jacket and tied the sleeves back around her waist. She smelled like a dog. "I wonder if Dad is still at the vet's. Maybe we should go in and call home." Her stomach tightened. What if Queen were dead?

"Queenie just can't die!" Paul twisted his hand in his jacket pocket. "Teddy Jo, I'll hate Dad forever if Queenie dies." Paul's voice was ragged with pain. "I'll come live with Grandpa."

"What's this about you coming to live with me?"

Teddy Jo turned with a gasp. "Grandpa!"

"You're home!" Paul leaped at Grandpa and hugged him hard around the wide waist. He smelled like peppermints and something different that Paul couldn't describe but it reminded him of his mother's perfume.

Teddy Jo darted a look toward the house. Anna wasn't in sight. Had Grandpa left her with her own family?

Grandpa looked over Paul's head at Teddy Jo. He smiled and his eyes were soft with love. "Hello."

Teddy Jo hung back. "Hi."

"I missed you."

"Me, too." She wanted to run to him and hug him, but she couldn't move. What if he didn't love her any longer? What if Anna filled his life so completely that he didn't need her now?

"I see you brought me a sway-backed horse and a litter of puppies." Grandpa stood with one arm around Paul and his other arm free. Teddy Jo knew that's where she belonged, but she couldn't make the move until she knew for sure he wanted her there.

Paul quickly told about Smokey, then Teddy Jo told about Queen and the puppies. "We don't know if Dad's still at the vet."

Grandpa pushed his fingers through his gray hair. "You kids have had enough excitement to last a lifetime." He looked different dressed in navy slacks and a long-sleeved white shirt instead of his usual green or tan pants and work shirts.

"We're glad you're home," said Paul.

"Yes," said Teddy Jo around a tight lump in her throat.

Grandpa winked at her and her heart leaped. "You're too far away, Teddy Bear Jo."

She flew into his arms and he held her close and she hugged him so hard that her arms ached. His shirt felt smooth against her cheek and she could hear the *thud*, *thud* of his heart. "I'm so glad you're home, Grandpa!"

"I couldn't stay away a minute longer. I missed you too much." He chuckled deep in his chest. "It looks like if I'd been gone any longer, I'd have come back to a full place. I leave here with a squirrel with a broken leg and a blackbird with a broken wing and come back to five little puppies and a black horse who wants to eat everything in sight."

"Before the day is over you might have a big gold collie." Teddy Jo's eyes sparkled as she looked up into Grandpa's dear face.

"We named her Queen, Grandpa." Paul slipped his small hand into Grandpa's large, rough hand. "Do you like that name?"

He nodded. "That I do."

"I wonder who dropped her off in the woods." Teddy Jo shook her head. "Who could be so mean? If I had a dog like Queen, I'd never let her go away from me—and I sure wouldn't drop her off to go wild!"

"Maybe whoever dropped her off thought

she'd go to a farm and find a home." Grandpa rubbed Teddy Jo's back. "Let's go inside and call the vet and see how Queen is."

Teddy Jo hesitated. If she went inside she'd see Anna and have to speak to her. Maybe Anna would expect a hug and a kiss.

Before Teddy Jo could refuse to go inside, Grandpa caught her hand and she couldn't pull free without making a scene. Meekly she walked with him and Paul practically danced along on the other side. He loved Anna and her cocker spaniel Honey. He was glad that they were going to be living with Grandpa.

Grandpa pushed open the back door and smells of hot cocoa and sweet rolls filled the air, and Teddy Jo's stomach grumbled with hunger. She frowned and pulled her stomach in until her rib cage stuck out. But still she was hungry and that usually sent her temper flaring.

"Hello, Paul." Anna held out her arms and Paul ran to her and hugged her.

Teddy Jo wanted to turn and run, but she leaned against the counter near the sink and crossed her arms.

"Hello, Teddy Jo. I'm glad to see you again." Anna didn't try to hug her and Teddy Jo was relieved. Grandpa wouldn't like it if she pushed Anna away.

"We found the puppies," said Paul excitedly. He went into great detail and Teddy Jo walked around the warm kitchen impatiently.

Finally Grandpa said, "I'll go call the vet."

Teddy Jo followed him to the phone. She leaned against him as he sat down and dialed the number, then waited while he talked. Her breath hurt her lungs and her legs trembled weakly.

Slowly Grandpa replaced the beige receiver and slipped his arms around Teddy Jo. His warm breath fanned her face. "Queen is hurt badly. She'll live, but she'll take a lot of care. The vet wants to keep her one, maybe two days and then your dad will bring her here."

"Oh!" Teddy Jo leaned against Grandpa and tears filled her eyes. "I hate Dad! He shot Queen even after we told him not to."

Grandpa held her for a while, then pushed her far enough away that he could look into her pale face. "Don't hate him, Teddy Jo. Hate only hurts you. Forgive your dad and love him. That's what Jesus wants you to do."

Teddy Jo bit her bottom lip, then barely nodded. Grandpa must never find out that she really wouldn't forgive or love Dad. Maybe someday if Queen lived and became a pet, then she might consider forgiving Dad. Maybe.

"Your dad is going home now and he wants you and Paul home. I said I'd take you after we check on the animals again."

"I want to stay here with you." Then she remembered Anna. "But I should go home."

"It really would be better. I know your dad is feeling bad. He's been trying to get close to you kids. I believe before long he'll accept Jesus as his personal Savior."

Teddy Jo looked down at her toes and a cold clamp seemed to tighten around her heart. Right now she didn't care if Dad ever became a Christian. Oh, what a bad, bad girl she was!

Abruptly she pulled away from Grandpa before he could read her mind. He had said that God had set her free so that she didn't have to do any bad things again. But what if Grandpa was wrong?

Frantically Teddy Jo dashed from the house and didn't stop until she was standing over the puppies in the shed. Her thin chest rose and fell and tears pricked the backs of her eyes. If Grandpa knew how bad she was, he wouldn't want to have anything to do with her.

Would God feel that same way?

She bowed her head and moaned.

A large hand closed over her arm and she peeked up at Grandpa. He bent down and kissed her flushed cheek. "What's bothering you, Teddy Bear Jo?"

Giant tears filled her eyes and she quickly ducked her head.

The puppies squirmed and whimpered. Smokey nickered. A car rattled past on the dirt road in front of the house.

Grandpa lifted her chin with his large hand. His hazel eyes were full of love and under-standing. "Just remember that you have a heavenly Father who will help you love and forgive. You are never on your own. He is always with you to help you and love you. His strength is yours if you just depend on it."

A sob escaped. "Oh, Grandpa!" She flung her arms around him and pressed her forehead into his chest and sobbed brokenly.

"Don't let your feelings rule you, Teddy Jo. The Bible says that we should live by faith and not make decisions according to how terrible things appear to be around us. God's Word says to forgive and love. Not if you *feel* like it. You just do it out of obedience. And as you obey, your feelings will line up with your actions. You'll begin to feel like you've forgiven your dad. You'll begin to feel love for him." Grandpa pulled out his large white hanky and wiped away her tears. "Satan is trying to win this battle. But you can't let him. He is your enemy and he is always at work trying to trouble you. But he can't unless you let him. Jesus already defeated him, so the fight is won. You just have to remember that."

Finally she nodded. "I do forgive Dad." She forced the words out. "With God's love I'll love him." Oh, but she didn't want to! He deserved her anger. But it wasn't right to feel that way either. She knew that she wasn't to judge or condemn.

Finally a peace settled in her heart and she smiled.

"Let's feed the puppies," said Grandpa.

"Let's," she said with a nod.

6
Dad's Gifts

With quick, deft strokes Teddy Jo drew Queen
on the heavy white drawing paper. She drew
the big collie as she'd looked before Dad had
shot her and not the weak, tired dog she was
now. Grandpa had said the day they'd brought
Queen home, "We'll have her back on her
feet in no time. Already she's less afraid than
she was." Dad hadn't said anything, but he
had bought a large bag of the finest dog food
as well as a bag of puppy chow.

Teddy Jo looked out her bedroom window
at the rain. Two hours ago she and Paul had
walked home from school in the cold rain.
Linda had caught a ride with a high school
friend.

Did Smokey mind the rain? Grandpa had
said that soon he'd be strong enough to ride.

Teddy Jo stretched Smokey beside Queen
and then she drew herself on Smokey's back.
She smiled and nodded. Soon she would ride

Smokey around the yard and Queen would run along beside them. After a while she'd let Paul have a turn. She squared her shoulders and lifted her chin. She might even let Paul go first.

The doorknob turned and she looked toward her door. How dare Paul walk in without knocking first! But it wasn't Paul. It was Dad! Never had he walked into her bedroom! Something in his face made her heart beat faster.

Paul sidled in and stood quietly beside the yellow and white bed. Dad had made him come in too. He knew Teddy Jo wouldn't like it, but there hadn't been anything he could do. He looked sideways at Dad, wondering what he wanted and why he insisted that he see both of them at the same time.

Teddy Jo waited, her hands locked on her drawing, her pencil beside her hand.

"I'm not going to bite you," said Larry with a scowl. "You two kids act like I'm poison or something."

"Sorry," said Teddy Jo tightly.

"I came to give you something, and Paul too." Larry held out a paper bag to Teddy Jo and another one to Paul.

Paul turned the bag over. What would Dad give him? It wasn't his birthday nor was it Christmas. Was he expected to say thank you? Was it even anything he wanted? Maybe it was a joke of some kind.

Teddy Jo looked from Dad to Paul, then to the bag in her hand.

"Well, aren't you going to open them?" Larry backed against the doorframe and waited, a half smile on his usually sober face.

Teddy Jo looked down at her drawing, and Dad said stiffly, "Can't you keep your nose out of your art for one minute? I want you to see what I got you."

Awkwardly Teddy Jo opened the bag and pulled out a soft-covered book. Her eyes widened in surprise. *"All about Horses,"* she read in a voice full of amazement.

"All about Dogs," whispered Paul as he stared at the paperback book with a picture of a large collie on the front of it.

"Thank you, Dad," Teddy Jo finally said. She saw the pleased look on his face and when Paul said thank you, he nodded, then turned and walked out, closing the door behind him.

Teddy Jo slumped back in her chair. "What a surprise! A book on horses!"

"And on dogs!" Paul held up his book. He could probably read it all tonight if the words weren't too long. Maybe Grandpa would read it to him after school tomorrow.

Teddy Jo flipped the pages and tried to look at the whole book at a glance. Would she be able to read it and understand it? Did Dad know that she had trouble reading sixth grade reading? Slowly she turned the pages to get a better look at the pictures. Someday she'd

be able to paint so well that her pictures would
be in books. She compared her picture with
one in the book, then quickly erased her
horse's ears and redrew them.

Paul flopped on his stomach on the soft
carpet and slowly looked at the dogs and read
the captions under the pictures. He'd teach
his dog to come and to sit and to stand on
command. They'd play together in the yard,
then sleep together in his room. Nobody would
make his dog leave his side.

Once again the bedroom door opened.
Teddy Jo's head snapped up and Paul pushed
himself to his knees.

"Hi, Mom," said Teddy Jo hesitantly.

Carol stood in the doorway, then slowly
walked in. She was dressed in a warm green
sweater and black slacks. Her dark brown hair
hung in curls around her face and onto her
slender shoulders. Her eyes were the same
shade of blue as Paul's. "I see you have the
books."

"Yes," said Teddy Jo, and Paul nodded.

Carol's diamond ring flashed as she locked
her fingers together. "Dad wanted to say
he was sorry about Queen. He wanted to do
something to please both of you. He hasn't
learned yet that he can tell you that he made
a mistake and that he's sorry. But he is sorry.
And now he's thankful that Queen is getting
better every day." She swallowed hard. "Could
you two try harder with Dad? He wants to

be part of your lives. He wants to make up for the past."

Teddy Jo stared at the soft gold carpet and Paul hunched his shoulders and clutched his book to his thin chest.

Mom walked to the bed and sank to the edge. "Come here, kids." She patted the spread on either side of herself. "Let's talk."

Teddy Jo licked her dry lips and slowly walked to the bed. She liked to have Mom come in and talk with her, but today seemed different.

Paul moved as close to Carol as he could. He liked the faint smell of her perfume but he knew Teddy Jo hated it. Perfume made her sneeze.

"Well, kids, there has been quite a change in our family since you both were born again. I am, and soon Linda and Dad will be. We are going to be a happy Christian family and not a torn apart group of people who fight all the time. We've prayed for our family and so has Grandpa and our prayers are being answered."

"Yes," said Teddy Jo.

"That's right," whispered Paul.

"Dad was very surprised that you forgave him for shooting Queen. Just continue to love him and pray for him. Ask him to go to Grandpa's with you sometime to see the dog and horse again."

Teddy Jo stiffened. Could she do that?

Paul twisted the tail of his blue shirt around

his finger. What if Dad got mad and made him stop playing with the puppies? What if he said they couldn't ride Smokey now that he was healthy enough?

"I know he won't go without an invitation from you." Carol squeezed Teddy Jo's thin shoulder. "I know you're full of God's love, Teddy Jo. And you, too, Paul. Share it with Dad. Don't be afraid. He needs us and he needs God. Dad won't be really happy until he's a Christian, and we all can let God's love shine through so he can see it."

"I'll try to ask if he wants to go with us tomorrow after school," said Paul, nodding his head hard.

"Me, too," said Teddy Jo weakly.

"Dad's popping corn and I told him I'd bring you back to the kitchen to have some."

"Is there cheese to sprinkle on it?" asked Paul as he jumped up. "I want that yellow cheese on it."

Mom laughed and quickly hugged Paul. "There's cheese."

Slowly Teddy Jo followed them out of her bedroom. Her life was almost perfect since Mom had become a Christian last year. Before then Mom had never held her close or kissed her or said she loved her. It would sure be funny to have Dad act that way. Mostly he yelled at them when they got noisy if he was watching TV.

Larry turned from the stove with a smile.

The kitchen smelled of popcorn and melted margarine. Glasses of iced Vernor's sat on the table. "The popcorn is ready. Maybe we could all play a game of Monopoly."

"That'll be fun," said Carol. She shot a warning look at Teddy Jo and Paul. "I'd better go tell Linda again that the popcorn's ready. She was on the phone and she probably forgot that I told her."

Teddy Jo took the dish of popcorn from Dad, then sat at the table and sprinkled cheese on it. "I like the horse book, Dad."

He beamed with pleasure. "I'm glad."

"I like the dog book, too," said Paul. He stuffed his mouth full of popcorn. It was nice and salty and loaded with cheese. With his mouth full he wouldn't have to say anything more to Dad.

Teddy Jo took a deep breath, then lost her courage. She couldn't say another word to Dad. She pushed popcorn into her mouth, then sipped the Vernor's.

Larry poured fresh popped corn into the large bowl, then slowly dripped margarine over it. "I saw those books in the variety store and I said to myself that you two would sure like them. So I bought them. I guess they'll help you a lot with that horse and those dogs."

Teddy Jo nodded. Mom and Linda walked in and Linda smelled like a perfume factory and looked like a TV ad for makeup. Teddy Jo wrinkled her nose and leaned back in her chair, glad that she didn't have to think of anything more to say to Dad.

Maybe tomorrow she'd say to him, "Hey, Dad, want to go to Grandpa's with us?" Maybe.

7
Roger Peck

"Queen looks almost well, doesn't she, Teddy Jo?" Paul pressed his nose against the wire fence of the kennel. The big gold collie just stood near the wooden doghouse and looked back at them. Her coat was almost as shiny as before she'd been shot. Her stance was just as proud. Paul's hands itched to stroke her, but Grandpa had said that they must not go inside the kennel.

"I bet she still misses her pups." Teddy Jo hunched inside her jacket as a cold wind blew, whipping leaves around the yard and knocking the last stubborn black walnuts from the trees. It felt almost cold enough to snow. And she hated to think of snow and cold weather because of Queen and Smokey. But Grandpa had showed her how thick their winter hair was getting and she felt better.

Paul looked toward the shed where he knew

the puppies were sleeping in a tight ball. He could play with them and they played back, finally without any fear. One of these days he'd ask Dad if he could have one and Dad would say of course he could, that every boy should have a dog of his own. He pulled his black knit hat over his cold ears and peeked up at Teddy Jo. Did she know what he was thinking? Maybe she was thinking the same thing. She wanted a dog as much as he did. One part of her bedroom wall was covered with her drawings of dogs. Sometimes he'd just stand and stare at them until they felt alive to him, then he'd have an adventure with them. It was better than watching TV.

"I wish Grandpa were here so he could help us ride Smokey again." Teddy Jo pushed her cold hands into her jacket pockets as she watched the black horse eating hay that she'd tossed in when she'd first come.

Paul took a deep breath. "We could ride by ourselves," he said quickly as if it were one word.

Teddy Jo's eyes widened. Had Paul really suggested such a daring thing? "You wouldn't do it even if I did, Paul."

He puffed out his thin chest. "I would too!"

"I'll bet."

Paul squared his shoulders and marched right for the pen. He'd sure show Teddy Jo! Wouldn't she ever learn that he wasn't a baby? He opened the gate and his hands trembled.

Smokey lifted his head and nickered.

"Paul!" Teddy Jo ran to the gate, laughing and shaking her head. "You can't fool me, Paul. You'll back out at the last minute." Excitement ran over her nerve ends and it was hard to stand still.

Paul's hand closed around the halter and Smokey meekly walked with him to the gate and out into the yard. "Get the saddle, Teddy Jo." He felt ten feet tall and as strong as Grandpa.

"I can't carry it and we're both too weak to put it on." She couldn't believe Paul. Was he as serious about this as he looked?

"Then we'll ride bareback. Get the bridle. I can stand on the bench and put it on." Was he really doing this? His stomach fluttered and he almost ran back inside the pen with Smokey, but instead he slowly walked to the bench that Grandpa always sat on when he watched them play.

Teddy Jo bit her bottom lip, then ran to the shed and lifted the bridle off the hook near the door. Shivers of excitement ran up and down her back. Would they really climb on Smokey's back and ride? Well, if Paul wasn't serious, then she'd just ride alone and let him stand in the yard and envy her.

Without a word Paul took the bridle and slipped it on Smokey. He turned the horse sideways to the bench, then slowly pulled himself onto Smokey's back. He grinned down at Teddy Jo, loving the astonished look on her face.

She jumped up on the bench, then scrambled behind Paul, hanging on around his waist. She felt taller than Grandpa's trees, almost as tall as the gray blue clouds in the sky.

Paul kicked Smokey's sides with his heels and said, "Get up." That's what Grandpa said when he rode Smokey. "Get up." The reins filled his hands. The wind seemed stronger and colder this far off the ground.

Smokey walked across the yard and Paul thought he was going to fall off. Wouldn't Teddy Jo laugh if that happened? He clung tighter to the reins.

Teddy Jo laughed at the sheer pleasure of riding Smokey. She never wanted to get off. Even when Smokey walked across the road and onto state property, she didn't say to stop and go back. She didn't want to go back. She wanted to ride and ride. This was better than anything she'd daydreamed, better than any of the stories she'd made up with Paul. Oh, wait'll she told Grandpa!

A cold band squeezed her heart. This was something she couldn't tell him. Well, then, she just wouldn't tell. He didn't need to know every part of her life. She sure didn't know all about his. She didn't know where he'd taken Anna for dinner, except that it was in Grand Rapids and that they'd be home late.

Smokey walked along the path in the woods

as if he were used to carrying two kids bareback. The trees helped cut off the sharp wind. Paul wanted to turn Smokey and go back to Grandpa's yard, but he couldn't without a tree branch knocking them to the ground. As soon as they reached a clearing, he'd turn Smokey and go home. Teddy Jo would never know how scared he was. And he sure wouldn't tell her!

Finally he spotted the Peck's deserted place and he sighed in relief. They could get down and rest awhile, then ride home. His bottom hurt and his legs felt out of joint.

A whirlwind of dried leaves blew across the Peck's driveway, then caught against the side of the house in another pile of leaves and weeds.

Just as Paul stopped Smokey, the door of the house burst open and Roger Peck ran out.

Teddy Jo gasped, suddenly frightened by the wild look on Roger's face. Why was he here again? He and his dad had moved away. Linda didn't know about his return or the whole family, the whole world, would've known.

"Get off my horse right now! I could get you Miller kids tossed into jail for stealing my horse!" The wind whipped Roger's dirty hair around his head and across his face. He pushed it aside and held it back. He wore ragged jeans and a jacket that looked like it once had belonged to his dad. It hung loosely around him and had only one button.

"We found Smokey in your shed starving to death," said Teddy Jo in a crisp voice. "We saved his life! Get away and let us ride back home."

Paul huddled into himself, his eyes wide and his heart pumping hard and fast. Why didn't he just kick Roger out of the way and ride like the wind back to Grandpa's? But he couldn't get the message to his foot.

Roger gripped the bridle. "Get off my horse right now!"

"So you can starve him to death again?" cried Teddy Jo, glaring down at him.

"I told Chad Lakin to come over every day and feed and water Smokey until we could come get him and take him with us."

"Chad Lakin! All he knows how to do is smoke pot!" Teddy Jo nudged Paul and hissed in his ear, "Let's get out of here."

Paul wanted to, but he couldn't move and if he tried, he knew Roger would do something terrible to him.

"Don't think you can leave on my horse!" Roger easily pried Paul's hands open and pulled out the reins. "Now get down!"

Paul clutched Smokey's mane and hung on tightly. Tears pricked his eyes and he ducked his head. He sure was a baby and he might as well admit it to himself and not pretend that he was anything else. He should wear Pampers and suck a bottle.

Teddy Jo swung down and landed beside Roger with a thud. Her feet stung and her temper flared. "You don't deserve to have a horse! We found him tied in that shed." She pointed with her arm out straight. "And he was dying! We took him home and took care of him all the time you've been gone." She narrowed her eyes and stuck her fists on her hips and stood with her feet apart. "Just why are you back? You said you wouldn't be back."

He wrinkled his nose. "I don't have to answer to you, Teddy Jo Miller. You're nothing but a kid."

"You sure have to tell me why you left your horse to die!"

"I told you I had somebody taking care of him."

She shook her finger in his face. "Well, he was starving!"

Paul slowly, carefully slipped off Smokey. His mouth felt bone-dry and his legs trembled weakly.

"Smokey is my horse and you can't do anything about that, so just run home."

Teddy Jo stamped her foot. "I'll . . . I'll tell Linda! She'll know just what you're like and she'll never go out with you again!"

Roger's face darkened. "Leave Linda out of this. It's our fight and not hers." He stepped toward Teddy Jo menacingly and she backed away. He was much taller and could hurt her easily and she knew it. "You take your brother and get out of here. Or you'll be very, very sorry."

Oh, but she wanted to stand up to Roger Peck and if she'd been a lot taller and stronger, she would have. She grabbed Paul's arm and jerked. "Let's get away from this horse killer! We don't want to catch any of his cruelty."

"One of these days your mouth is going to get you in over your head, Teddy Jo Miller." Roger turned Smokey and led him toward the shed.

Teddy Jo's face flushed hotly and she ran with Paul away from Peck's property. Somehow she'd get Smokey away from Roger Peck and she'd do it before Roger mistreated him.

Smokey whinnied as if he were in pain.

Teddy Jo twirled around, her heart racing. She had to get Smokey away from Roger now! But how could she?

8
Dad to the Rescue

Teddy Jo pressed her hand to her forehead and
sank to the bench in Grandpa's backyard.
"He said he'd be right here!"

"Dad?" Paul twisted around on the bench,
his eyes wide in surprise. "But he'll miss that
sportsman's show on TV!"

"I know, but he said he'd be right over. He
said to sit tight and he'd come help us. He
said that." Teddy Jo pulled her knees up to her
cold chin and wrapped her arms around her
legs. The wind had died down and the sun was
trying to peek through the clouds.

"How can he get Smokey away from Roger
Peck? If Grandpa were home, he could, but
Dad? I sure don't know about Dad."

Teddy Jo narrowed her eyes. Anna Sloan
was to blame for Grandpa being gone. He sure
wouldn't have gone to Grand Rapids to eat
alone. He'd be right here when they needed
his help. She wriggled uncomfortably. If they

hadn't ridden Smokey, they wouldn't be in this trouble right now. She quickly pushed that disturbing thought aside and listened for Dad's pickup. When she finally heard it she ran around the garage and stopped uncertainly.

"What's wrong?" asked Paul, tugging his hat lower over his ears. His face was red with cold.

"What if he says that Smokey belongs to Roger and won't help at all?" Teddy Jo eyed Dad as he strode toward them, his winter coat swinging open. He was dressed in worn jeans and a blue sweat shirt, a darker shade of blue than his eyes. His dark hair was uncombed and covered his ears and touched his collar.

"What was so desperate that you couldn't handle it alone?" Larry asked gruffly.

"It's Smokey," said Teddy Jo, and Paul nodded hard.

"Is he sick?"

"He's gone!" The words burst from her, then she forced herself to calm down a little and she told him what had happened. He studied them both for several seconds, his eyes narrowed, his lips pressed tightly together.

Finally he cleared his throat. "I know it won't do a bit of good to tell you that you weren't supposed to ride Smokey when Ed was gone."

70

Paul ducked his head and Teddy Jo bit her bottom lip.

"What's done is done. We can't leave that horse with the Pecks or he'll end up the way he was when you first found him." Larry motioned to the pickup. "Get in and wait for me. I'll get the saddle and you two will just have to ride that horse back here."

"Oh!" said Paul.

Teddy Jo couldn't speak at all. Dad sounded so sure of himself. How was he going to get Smokey from them? Roger was bigger than Dad and so was Mr. Peck.

Several minutes later Larry stopped the pickup beside the old brown pickup that stood outside the run-down house. Smoke rolled from the brick chimney. The yard was deserted.

"You two can stay here if you want." Larry opened the door and cold air rushed in.

Teddy Jo pushed her door open and dropped to the ground, then Paul almost fell out beside her. They ran around and caught up with Larry just as he knocked loudly on the door.

The door burst open and Roger Peck stood there, his dark brows almost meeting over his long nose. He swore angrily, his eyes boring into Teddy Jo's. She knew he was blaming her for any more trouble. "What do you want?"

"Tell your dad I want to see him." Larry sounded calm and didn't look at all scared and

Teddy Jo felt a stirring of pride deep inside her.

"What is it you want, Miller?" Mr. Peck pushed Roger aside and glared at Larry. Father and son looked very much alike, both ragged and dirty and unkept. And angry at the intrusion.

Paul moved closer to Larry, ready to help if the Pecks started a fight.

"Your boy is in a lot of trouble because of that horse of his." Larry looked the man right in the eye. "I don't think you want the trouble of going to court over it, do you?" Larry pulled out his worn wallet. "I want to buy the horse from you."

Teddy Jo's mouth fell open.

Roger swore. "I don't want to sell."

"Keep your mouth shut!" Mr. Peck cuffed Roger, then turned back to Larry. "He don't want to sell."

"Listen, Al. You and me have worked at the same factory for almost a year now. Word gets around."

Al Peck's face turned a brick red and he cleared his throat nervously. "So?"

"So, I'm ready to offer you a good price for that horse."

Teddy Jo's heart leaped. Would Dad really pay out his hard-earned money for Smokey? Would that mean Smokey would actually belong to them?

"We can't stand here talking in the cold," said Al Peck gruffly. "We'll settle this inside. Roger, clean off them chairs so we can sit down."

Roger flushed and quickly scraped clothes and newspapers off the chairs that stood around a square table cluttered with dirty dishes, leftover food, and a pair of dirty socks. "You can't have my horse," he said in a low, mean voice to Teddy Jo. "You'll never get him!"

"Shut your yap!" Al Peck pushed Roger aside and sank to one of the chairs. "Sit down, Miller, and let's get this settled here and now."

Larry sat down and Teddy Jo and Paul huddled behind his chair while Roger dropped down on the only other chair.

"I'll give you twenty-five dollars for the horse," said Larry as he dropped a twenty and a five on the table next to a plate smeared with egg yolk.

"I'd shoot the thing first!" Al Peck leaned forward, his large hands clamped over his legs just above the knees.

Fear pricked Teddy Jo's skin. She knew the man meant what he said. She darted a look at Roger and she knew he was just as fearful as she.

"That's all I'm offering, Al. Take it or I'll drop my price."

"I paid more for him than that!"

"If I added up what you owe Ed Korman

and my kids for feeding him and keeping him the past few weeks, then you'd be out even this twenty-five dollars."

"I'm not selling," said Roger sullenly.

Al Peck glared at him and he dropped his head and closed his mouth tightly. "You raise that price and I'll consider your offer, Miller."

Larry shook his head. "I think I'll make a phone call to Mr. Sawyer and tell him that you're back in town. Then we'll go from there."

Al's face turned redder, then blanched. "The horse is yours. Just get him out of here today and stay off my property or you'll be very sorry."

Larry scraped back his chair and Teddy Jo and Paul jumped back. "We'll take the horse now. Roger has Ed's bridle, too."

"Get it for them," said Al, pushing Roger toward the door.

"Write me out a bill of sale and we'll be on our way," said Larry as he handed Al a pen.

Al hunted around for a piece of paper, then angrily ripped the bottom off a letter and wrote out a bill of sale and tossed it at Larry. He caught it and handed it to Teddy Jo.

She clutched it tightly, her eyes full of questions. Finally she pushed it into her pocket and walked outdoors with Dad and Paul. Was Smokey really theirs?

Several minutes later Teddy Jo and Paul sat in the saddle on Smokey's back. Roger stood nearby, his face white and his eyes full of pain.

"You kids be careful," said Larry. "I'll wait at Grandpa's for you." He climbed in his pickup and drove away.

"I'll get Smokey back," said Roger in a voice that made Teddy Jo shudder.

Teddy Jo nudged Smokey and walked him away from Peck's property onto state land. She couldn't forget the sadness in Roger's eyes.

"Smokey is ours," said Paul in awe. He clung tightly to Teddy Jo's waist and rested his cheek on her back. He felt snug and warm and happy.

"Wasn't Dad wonderful?"

"He didn't seem like our dad at all."

"When we get to Grandpa's I'm going to tell him thank you. I'm going to tell him that's the best thing I've ever seen."

Paul was quiet a long time, then he said, "Do you think Roger will try to get Smokey back? Do you think he'll steal him?"

Teddy Jo watched a squirrel jump from the top of one tree to another. She didn't want to think about Roger Peck or his threat. "Let's just enjoy the ride, Paul."

At Grandpa's she slid off Smokey, but before she could touch the ground, strong arms caught her and helped her land softly. She twisted her head to find Dad. Her heart leaped.

"I was getting a little worried," he said as he reached to help Paul dismount.

Paul rested his hands on Dad's shoulders,

then slid to the ground. "We had a good ride." He swallowed hard. "Is Smokey really for us?"

Larry nodded. "If Grandpa will keep him here."

"Oh, he will!" cried Teddy Jo. "Thanks, Dad!" She wanted to hug him, but she hung back, suddenly shy. "You got Smokey back and we're sure glad."

Larry flushed with pleasure. He squeezed Teddy Jo's shoulder and she wanted to touch his hand, but she stood very still, smiling up at him.

This was her dad and he was touching her and looking at her as if he loved her. Love for him rose inside of her until she thought she would burst.

Queen barked and Teddy Jo turned away from Dad to look toward the kennel.

"I think she's hungry," said Paul.

"Let's go feed her," said Larry.

"And the puppies, too," said Teddy Jo.

"I bet they grew a lot since I saw them last," said Larry.

Teddy Jo shot a look of surprise at Paul, then ran after Dad to take care of the dogs. There was sure a change in Dad. Pretty soon he'd be as nice as Grandpa.

9
An Angry Linda

"If I had to choose one out of these five, I'd take this one." Teddy Jo rubbed the tan and white puppy, then hugged it close. It stuck its cold nose against her warm neck. "See how its ears stick up like a German shepherd, Paul?"

"It's pretty, all right, but this one is my favorite. It's fat and furry and has some gold like its mother. I'll keep this one and I'll think of a great name for it." But no great name came to mind and he'd been thinking on it for days.

The sun shone warmly down on the puppies playing in the grass. Teddy Jo's jacket lay in a heap beside her. She finally gave up her favorite puppy and picked up another one just so none felt left out. She looked thoughtfully at Paul where he lay in the grass with the pups. "You know, Paul, yesterday Dad was nice and bought Smokey for us. Maybe today he'll

tell us that we can have a dog of our own." She
saw the unbelief on Paul's face. "He might,
you know."

Paul just shrugged. It was too beautiful of a
day to argue with Teddy Jo. It never got him
anywhere anyway.

Teddy Jo stretched out on the grass and
watched the puppies. She thought of the
drawing that she'd been working on. Had she
made the noses just right? She really should've
brought her pad and sketched the puppies
in action. Maybe the picture of the puppies
would be better to enter in the art festival than
the one of the doe and fawn. She really should
be home right now finishing the picture for
the art festival November fifteenth.

She sat up with a start. November fifteenth!
Oh, no! How could the art festival be on
that day? Why hadn't she realized before that
that was the first day of deer hunting and
that Dad and Mom were both going. They'd
never give up the first day of deer hunting for
her art festival. Nothing was more important
to them than deer hunting.

She groaned and Paul looked at her ques-
tioningly, but she couldn't tell him or she just
might burst into tears. Once again this year
her work was going to be honored because
she'd won the blue ribbon in the sixth grade
art. Now, her work would be judged with
fifth-graders through eighth-graders.

And Mom and Dad wouldn't be there to see

her display or hear the praise Mr. Palmer would give her. Maybe even Grandpa wouldn't be there if Anna didn't want to go. Maybe she'd end up standing beside her display with no family or no friends around to see her moment of glory.

She sank down lower in the grass and her wide mouth turned down at the corners. She might as well tell her teacher that she didn't want to display her work at the festival or even enter the picture that she'd painted to be judged.

At the sound of someone running, she looked up to find Linda running toward her. Linda's face was red and she looked ready to burst. Her eye makeup was smudged and her usually tidy hair was in tangles.

Paul saw her coming and he saw the anger in every line of her body. Slowly he pushed himself up and tried to look invisible. But she wasn't looking at him. She was heading right for Teddy Jo.

Linda stopped short, her chest heaving. "How dare you take Roger's horse, Teddy Jo! How dare you!"

Teddy Jo leaped up. "Roger! I should've known you'd take his side. You didn't see what he did to Smokey. You are only thinking about Roger Peck."

"Smokey belongs to Roger and you had no business talking Dad into buying him from Mr. Peck. Roger loves Smokey! He was planning on getting Smokey as soon as they were settled in Grand Rapids."

Teddy Jo flipped back her dark hair. "And just where would he keep Smokey? In the Woodland Mall?"

"He'd find a place. He's smart."

"Roger Peck? If he's so smart, why'd he pick you for a girl friend?" Teddy Jo wanted to grab the words back, but it was too late. She saw the hurt that was quickly masked with anger.

Linda rushed past Teddy Jo and stopped at the gate. She'd show Teddy Jo! Her fingers trembled awkwardly as she swung open the gate. Smokey ran to her and she stepped aside and he walked through the gate.

"Don't, Linda!" cried Teddy Jo, running toward the pen. She called over her shoulder. "Paul, take care of the puppies and help me get Smokey back in."

Smokey pranced away from Teddy Jo's grasp, then side-jumped.

"Easy, Smokey. Don't run away from me. I have some food and water for you."

Linda watched Teddy Jo try to coax Smokey back to the pen. Just as Teddy Jo thought she had him, Linda rushed at Smokey with a loud yell. Smokey spun around and ran toward the black walnut trees and Teddy Jo followed, shouting his name.

With a wicked chuckle Linda walked to the

kennel and flung wide the door. The big gold collie stood near the doghouse, eyeing her. "Get out, dog! I'm setting you free."

"Shut that door!" shouted Paul. "We'll never catch her if she gets out!"

Just then the back door of the house opened and Anna stepped out with Honey beside her. The cocker spaniel barked and ran toward Paul.

"What's going on out here?" shouted Anna, holding her white sweater around her well-rounded body.

"Get Grandpa!" shouted Paul frantically. He didn't know what to do first, so he just stood in the middle of the backyard and looked helplessly around. Honey sniffed his feet, then ran to the kennel and right through the gate.

"Stop her, Linda!" cried Anna, running toward them. "Queen will kill Honey. Why did you open that gate? What's gotten into you?"

Teddy Jo heard the shouting behind her, but she kept running after Smokey. How could Linda do such a terrible thing? What if Smokey ran right back to Roger Peck? She'd never get him back. Roger would sure see to that.

Branches caught at her hair as she ran. Her mouth turned dry and her lungs ached. Heat pricked her body.

"Smokey! Smokey!" She called just as she tripped on a root. She sprawled to the ground, the wind knocked out of her. Leaves scratched her face and the musty smell made her sneeze.

Slowly she pushed herself up, gasping for breath. She had to catch Smokey. That Linda was going to be one sorry girl when she got back! Linda had better start running now. How dare she turn Smokey loose!

Smokey nickered and Teddy Jo lifted her head in surprise. Smokey stood several feet away, watching her.

"I'm going to catch you and take you back to Grandpa's, Smokey. You don't have to be afraid and run from me. We're friends. Remember?" Slowly Teddy Jo got up and walked toward the dark horse. He tossed his head, but didn't run. Finally she slipped her hand through his halter, then just stood there with her forehead against his dusty neck. "I'm sorry that Linda scared you. Let's go back and get you a nice cool drink and a big pile of hay."

Slowly they walked back through the trees and finally reached the backyard. Teddy Jo stopped, her eyes wide in alarm.

Shouting, screaming, and wild barking reached her ears. As she watched, Queen tore into little Honey and tossed her high in the air. Teddy Jo froze, her stomach tightened with fear.

10
Anna Sloan Korman

Weakly, Teddy Jo leaned against Smokey and
watched the terrible scene in the kennel. Why
didn't someone stop Queen from fighting
with Honey? Was the little dog already dead?

Just then Grandpa ran to the kennel with a
long yellow water hose. He pushed the handle
and sprayed Queen. "Get away from that dog
right now, Queen! Go!" He walked closer, the
spray harder and colder, and Queen slunk back
and finally ran into the doghouse.

Anna lifted Honey and hurried from the
kennel. "How could you open that gate, Linda
Miller?"

Teddy Jo had never seen Anna angry, but
she was angry now and everyone came under
the lashing of her tongue.

"That dog shouldn't be allowed to live! It's
a wild dog and very dangerous." She lifted
angry brown eyes to Grandpa. "Ed, I am at my

wits' end. You send these kids home before I say something that can't be righted."

"Let me have a look at Honey." Grandpa held out his arms, but Anna shook her head hard and backed away.

"I am taking her to the vet and nothing had better be wrong with her!" She flashed a look around to Teddy Jo, Paul, Linda, then back to Grandpa. "She'd better live and be healthy. Or else!"

Grandpa clamped a large hand on Anna's shoulder. "Honey will be just fine. You go to the car and I'll be right there. I'm driving you to the vet. Don't say another word! I am driving you."

Teddy Jo knew that she wouldn't argue if he talked in that tone to her and Anna didn't either. She walked swiftly around the garage.

Linda watched her go and her heart almost burst with pain. She'd caused the fight between Queen and Honey. If anything happened to Honey it would be her fault. She moaned and walked to the bench and slumped down.

Paul rubbed the back of his hand across his nose and moved from foot to foot. He had to get to the bathroom before it was too late. He darted a look at Grandpa, then raced to the back door.

Teddy Jo slowly walked to the pen and turned Smokey inside. She locked the gate with trembling hands. Oh, how she wanted to leap on Linda and toss her up and away just like Queen did to Honey. Only Linda deserved it and Honey didn't.

With a sigh Teddy Jo carried water to Smokey, then stopped as Grandpa's large hand closed around her thin arm. She looked up and almost burst into tears. He looked sad and hurt and she wanted to slip her arms around him and comfort him.

"You kids finish here, then run on home. I'll call you to let you know how Honey is. But I prayed for her and I know she'll live." He looked toward Linda. "I don't want you to fight with Linda. She did this out of anger and pain and frustration. I'll talk to her later. You just love her and forgive her the way Jesus wants you to."

Teddy Jo rolled her eyes. How could she love and forgive Linda? Right now it was impossible to think about. She finished watering and feeding Smokey, then helped Paul do the rest of the chores. Linda was gone when they walked out of the shed.

"I hope she runs away from home," muttered Paul, his face white and his fists doubled. "She should be punished!"

Teddy Jo kicked a stone as they walked along the side of the dirt road. "Grandpa said he'd take care of it. And I bet Anna will, too. She sure was mad."

"I bet she loves Honey as much as she loves Grandpa. She's had Honey a long time."

A pickup drove past. A cool wind blew from the north, and Teddy Jo slipped her jacket on. Tears stung her eyes. She loved Honey and she knew Paul did too. Grandpa had said that he'd prayed for Honey and that she'd live.

"Thank you, Jesus, for making Honey all right," mouthed Teddy Jo. She knew Jesus cared about animals because she cared about them. He'd make Honey well. She blinked fast to clear her vision. No way would she cry in front of Paul. She heard a sniff and she glanced sideways at Paul to find him fighting against tears. She touched his arm and he looked up at her, his face flushing red. "Honey will be all right, Paul. She will."

Much later Teddy Jo stood beside Paul in their kitchen and told Mom and Dad what had happened.

"I wondered why Linda ran to her room crying," said Carol, looking thoughtfully toward the hall that led to the bedrooms.

"She won't ever see that Roger Peck again if I have anything to do about it," said Larry with a dark scowl. He sat at the table, a cup of coffee in front of him and a half-eaten tuna sandwich. "You're too easy with her, Carol."

Carol turned in a flash. "*I'm* too easy! *You're* the one who ignores her and lets her do what she wants."

Teddy Jo fled to her room. She sank to the edge of her room and covered her ears to keep from hearing the angry shouts. She knew Paul had slunk away either to watch TV or hide in his room until after the fight.

Finally Teddy Jo walked to her desk and looked down at the painting of the doe and fawn. She shook her head. This was sure not her day. Why even bother to become a great artist. Who would care? All her family wanted to do was fight.

She picked up the pile of drawings and slowly looked through them. A picture of Honey leaped out at her and she moaned. Oh, she dare not lose hope! She rubbed her finger across the drawing and managed to smile.

The doorknob turned and the door slowly opened. Teddy Jo stiffened, then frowned as Linda walked in. Her eyes were red from crying. Her blouse looked rumpled and her jeans dirty. She looked nothing like the usual beauty queen that she tried to be all the time.

"Have you heard anything about Honey yet?" Linda's voice broke and she looked down at the soft carpet.

Teddy Jo's heart swelled with compassion and she walked to Linda and touched her arm. "We prayed for Honey. She'll be all right. You'll see. Grandpa and Anna will walk in and tell us that Honey is as good as new."

Linda smiled weakly. "Do you really think so?"

"Yes."

"Teddy Jo?"

"What?"

"I am sorry about today. I am!"

Teddy Jo took a deep breath. "I know."

"I love Roger so much and I hated to have him hurt. I told him that I'd help get Smokey back for him, but I know I can't. He's going back to Grand Rapids and he said I could take care of Smokey while he was gone." Linda shook her head. "Can you see me doing that even for Roger? I am going to tell him that Smokey is better off where he is and that if he's nice to you, you'll let him ride Smokey once in a while."

"I guess I could do that." She remembered the pain in Roger's eyes. "He probably won't accept that, but we *will* let him ride Smokey once in a while." She looked down at her stocking feet, then finally up at Linda. "I'm sorry for saying bad things to you before. They just popped out."

"I know. That's what happens to me too." She walked to the desk and noticed the art for the first time. "Did you do these, Teddy Jo?"

She nodded. "You've seen my work before."

"Not for a long time. I heard some of the kids talking about the art festival and I knew you'd be entering, but I didn't know you were this good."

The words warmed Teddy Jo's heart and she pulled out the picture with the blue ribbon on it. "I won this."

"You did?" She held the picture and studied

it. "I sure wish I could do this. I can't do anything that's worth doing."

Teddy Jo heard the despair in Linda's voice, but she didn't know what to say to help her. It was funny to have Linda envious of her.

Just then someone knocked and Teddy Jo said, "Come in."

Grandpa and Anna walked in with Honey padding along beside them. Anna smiled hesitantly and Grandpa winked.

"Honey!" Linda dropped to her knees and hugged the small dog.

"I'm glad she's all right," said Teddy Jo, looking uncertainly at Anna.

Anna cleared her throat and looked from Teddy Jo to Linda. Paul walked in and she caught him to her and hugged him, tears sparkling in her eyes. Finally she released him and he dropped beside Linda and Honey.

"Kids," said Anna in a low voice. "I am very sorry for yelling at you. I was upset and I was scared." She rested her hand on Linda's shoulder and finally Linda jumped up and wrapped her arms around Anna.

Teddy Jo stood alone, fighting against a strange feeling inside. Part of her wanted to walk into Anna's arms and part of her wanted to be angry at Anna.

Grandpa rubbed his hand along her cheek and she turned her face into his work-roughened hand. "You have enough love for your new grandma, Teddy Jo," he said for her ears alone.

She pulled back stiffly and once again stood alone, her hands locked behind her back.

Teddy Jo's Gift

Grandpa held up the drawing of Honey. "You did a fine job here, Teddy Jo. Look, Anna."

Teddy Jo frowned at Grandpa for making the other notice her artwork, but he didn't pay attention to her. He calmly handed the sheaf of papers to Anna and she looked through them, exclaiming softly every so often.

Paul sat on the bedroom floor with Honey on his lap. Why should they think Teddy Jo was so great just because she could draw? If he wanted to he could draw better than any artist alive or dead.

Linda stood quietly beside Anna, her head down. Jealousy surged inside and she wanted to do something, anything, to make Anna and Grandpa notice her. But she couldn't think of anything to do or say.

Finally Anna stepped toward Teddy Jo. "You have a wonderful gift, Teddy Jo. It's a gift

91

from God and you are using it well. Continue
drawing and painting. Your grandpa told me
that you have an art festival coming up. That's
very exciting for you. We want to be there
to share your day." The blue sweater she wore
made her eyes more blue than green. Her
graying hair was cut short and combed back off
her face. "You sure are an artist, Teddy Jo."

Teddy Jo knew Anna was sincere and she
smiled slightly. Why couldn't she say something back that would make Anna know that
the kind words pleased her?

"Did you show your mom and dad your
work?" asked Grandpa.

Teddy Jo licked her dry lips. "I couldn't."

"I know they'd be proud of your skill," said
Anna.

Linda stepped forward. "Anna, I got new
makeup. Would you come see it?"

Ann turned to her with a wide smile. "I'd
love to, Linda. I want to see your new sweater
that you told me about."

Teddy Jo sagged with relief when Anna
walked out. Honey ran after her and Paul
followed.

"She's a wonderful person, Teddy Jo," said
Grandpa softly. "She won't push herself onto
you. You liked her just fine before she became
Anna Korman. She's the same person."

"I know." Teddy Jo caught Grandpa's large
hand and held it firmly. "I don't know what's
wrong with me."

Grandpa kissed her flushed cheek and winked. "Nothing's wrong with you, honey. You're full of love and it'll flow out if you just let it."

Just then Larry poked his head in. "Carol has coffee ready in the kitchen if you want a cup, Ed."

"Thanks, Larry." Grandpa walked to the door. "This girl of yours has a wonderful gift. I know you must really be proud of her."

Teddy Jo wanted to sink through the floor. Dad didn't want to know about her talent and he sure wasn't proud of her.

Larry glanced toward the desk, then slowly walked to it as Grandpa hurried to the kitchen for a cup of coffee. "When did you start drawing, Teddy Jo?"

She flushed and her mouth felt too dry to answer. She'd always drawn and he should know that. "I've worked on these for about two weeks now."

Larry found the painting with the blue ribbon on it. "And what is this?" He sounded as if he were accusing her of something terrible and she hung back, flushing hotly.

"I won the sixth grade art award," she managed to say around her tight throat. She'd told both Mom and Dad the day she'd won, but they'd been busy talking about their jobs.

"Why haven't you said anything about it?"

She shrugged. Why say anything now?

"I heard Anna mention an art festival to

Mom. What's that all about?" Larry stood with one hand on the back of her chair and the other on his hip.

Briefly she told about the festival and that her work was being honored. "This is what I painted for this festival." Her voice sounded stiff and not at all like herself.

"When is the festival?"

She looked out the window at the darkening sky. "Next Friday," she said barely above a whisper.

"Is everyone invited or is it a closed show?"

Her heart leaped and she looked up at Dad in surprise. "It's for everyone."

"You do have a gift for art. I had an uncle who was quite an artist. He never did much with it, but he could sure paint. Horses, he painted, and apples in a basket." Larry pushed his hands into his jeans pockets and jingled his keys and change. "I want us to get to know each other, Teddy Jo. I'm trying and I want you to try."

Teddy Jo tugged at the neck of her sweater. "I'll try." What did he expect of her? Did he want her to talk about his job with him? Or maybe about hunting and fishing. She couldn't think of anything else that he ever talked about.

Larry picked up a picture of two rabbits playing around a fallen log. "I can see you'd rather draw a picture of a rabbit than shoot one." He flashed a teasing grin that surprised her. "I made a big mistake trying to take you and your brother hunting. But I learned, and I won't do it again. I was trying to make you part of my life, but I see that I'll have to fit myself into your life."

Teddy Jo trembled and tears stung her eyes. Was this really her dad talking to her? She pushed her dark hair out of her eyes. Dare she ask if he'd come to the art festival? She took a deep breath and pushed out the words. "I'd like you to come to the art festival Friday."

Larry nodded. "I will and I know your mother will."

Teddy Jo sank to the edge of the bed. "You will?"

"Why are you so surprised? I just said that I am interested in you."

She picked up her rag doll that Dara Cook had given her and hugged it close. "Friday is the fifteenth," she said hoarsely.

He frowned and looked back at the calendar on her desk. "The fifteenth?"

"Yes. The opening day of deer hunting."

He shook his head. "Oh, that's a shame. A real shame."

She wanted to throw herself against her pillow and sob at the top of her lungs. She *knew* that they wouldn't give up the first day of deer hunting for her.

With a sigh Larry walked to the doorway,

then stopped and looked back. "I'm sorry for hurting you, Teddy Jo, but you know how it is."

She nodded. She knew exactly how it was.

He walked out, then poked his head back in. "How long does the festival last?"

"Until three."

He pursed his lips. "I can't promise, but if we get our deer early, we'll come to the art festival."

Teddy Jo nodded again, her shoulders drooping. Dad would get his deer, then be so excited about it that he'd take it around tied to the pickup and show it off to all his friends. He'd forget all about her and her artwork.

"You do have a gift, Teddy Jo. A real gift, and I'm glad."

She watched him walk away, then she turned and pressed her face against her pillow and fought against the wild tears that threatened to fall.

12
The Art Festival

The crowd of school children along with
teachers and some parents who'd arrived early
buzzed around Teddy Jo in the high school
gym that had overnight turned into an arts
and crafts panorama. Shivers of excitement
ran up and down her spine and butterflies
fluttered in her stomach. She was dressed in
medium blue dress slacks with a long-sleeved
white sweater. Two blue barrettes held her
dark hair out of her face and made her eyes
look large and sparkly. She craned her neck
to see if she could spot someone she knew. Oh,
she dare not let herself think that Dad and
Mom would come. She'd watched them walk
out the door, dressed in red plaid coats with
guns in hands and licenses across their backs.
No, they wouldn't come.

She looked at the display behind her and all

her drawings and paintings suddenly looked ugly and crude. Why should anyone want to come see what she'd done? Why should she expect the judges to give her a ribbon of any kind? They might tell her that she had no business being here with her childish work.

Maybe Dad would get his buck early and come. The light snow that had fallen during the night had excited him. He said he could find deer tracks easier in the snow.

She sighed and wrapped her arms across her thin chest. She looked across the crowd, then gasped as she saw Linda with Roger Peck walking toward her. She didn't like the look on Roger's face and she turned away to find a way to escape them, but she had to stay with her display.

"Hello, Teddy Jo," said Linda coldly. She hadn't wanted to come, but Roger had insisted. He'd said that it was only right for a sister to see her sister's artwork. But she didn't want to see everyone paying attention to Teddy Jo, saying nice things to her and about her.

Teddy Jo slowly turned and lifted her chin. "Hi."

"Did you really get a blue ribbon for this?" asked Roger with a sneer. He flicked the picture and it rocked on its easel.

"Leave it alone," snapped Teddy Jo. She sure didn't need trouble from Roger Peck today.

He chuckled wickedly. "Look, Linda. She

drew a picture of Smokey. I think she should give it to me, don't you? She took my horse. I should take the drawing so I'll have something to remember him by." He tugged the stick pins out of the corkboard and pulled the picture off.

Teddy Jo stifled a scream as she grabbed for the picture. "That has to stay up there! It's part of my display!" She turned in despair to Linda. "Please make him stop!"

Linda shrugged. She hated to see Teddy Jo almost in tears, but she sure couldn't have everything her way.

"I said I'd get you for taking Smokey," said Roger. "Maybe I should take the picture of that wild dog. Better still, I should go let her go so you can't ever get her again." He laughed and Teddy Jo wanted to punch him in the nose.

How could she get the picture away from him? If she grabbed it, it would tear. And she couldn't allow him to walk away with it. The empty spot on her corkboard ruined the entire display.

"What's going on here?"

Teddy Jo sighed with relief to see Grandpa and Anna. He was looking very sternly at Roger, and Anna smiled reassuringly at Teddy Jo as she slipped her arm around Linda and said hello softly.

Linda wanted to disappear, but she stood close to Anna. Anna smelled like fresh air with a touch of rose perfume.

"Put the picture back, Roger," said Grandpa in a voice that anyone would obey. He stood a head taller than Roger and about seventy-five pounds heavier. "Do it now."

With a curse Roger threw the drawing at Teddy Jo, then pushed his way through several grade school children and disappeared.

With trembling hands Teddy Jo tacked the picture in place, then smiled tearfully up at Grandpa. "Thank you."

He winked at her and she caught his hand and squeezed it tightly.

"Anna saw what he'd done and she hurried me right over to rescue you." He smiled lovingly at Anna and she flushed and shrugged.

Teddy Jo turned stiffly to Anna. "Thank you."

"I'm glad we could help. Now, show us your work, will you? I am impressed at your beautiful display."

Linda pulled away from Anna and cleared her throat. "I'll see you later," She couldn't look at Teddy Jo. "I only have an hour in here, then I have to get to English class." She had to find Roger and make sure he wasn't mad at her.

Teddy Jo repeated her speech that she'd memorized to give to all the people who stopped and asked about her work.

"We'll be back to say good-bye before we leave," said Grandpa. "I don't think Roger will give you any more trouble today." He kissed her cheek and she flushed with pleasure, then looked quickly around to see if anyone had noticed.

Jane Brent stopped with a pleased smile. "Teddy Jo, your work is outstanding! I tell everyone that I live next door to a budding artist. Mike should be here, too. He said he never saw a girl who could play soccer so well as well as draw and paint."

"Thanks, Mrs. Brent."

"Are your parents here yet?" Jane Brent looked around with interest.

Teddy Jo looked down at her locked fingers. "No, not yet." She couldn't say aloud that they might not come. It would hurt too much.

Mrs. Brent talked a few more minutes, then walked on, making room for several others waiting to see Teddy Jo's work.

Teddy Jo's face hurt from smiling so much and her mouth was dry from answering questions and giving her speech. In a break in the crowd she hurried to the fountain and drank her fill of cold water. She rubbed the back of her hand across her mouth, then stopped and stood very still.

A man dressed in brown slacks and a tan pullover sweater was walking away from her and he walked just like Dad. He was short and slight like Dad and she almost called out to him. With a breathless laugh she hurried after him. Just as she reached out for his arm, he turned his head and she saw he had a full brown beard and her hand fell to her side. It wasn't Dad at all.

With her head down she walked back to her spot and once again recited her speech and smiled and nodded and answered questions.

At one o'clock Mr. Smelker stood at the mike and announced that the judges had reached a decision. Teddy Jo wiped her damp palms down her slacks and waited. She could hear her heart beating. She felt someone beside her and she looked up to find Dad standing there with Mom beside him.

"Did you get your deer?" Teddy Jo asked breathlessly.

"No," whispered Larry. "But we wanted to come see you and your work so we decided to wait and go out again in the morning."

"Shh," said Carol. "Let's hear the winners."

Teddy Jo felt as if she were floating on a fluffy cloud. Mom and Dad had actually given up hunting for the day to come see her and her artwork!

Suddenly Carol nudged Teddy Jo. "Go!"

"What?"

Larry chuckled. "The man just announced that you won the blue ribbon in your class of art. Don't you want to get it?"

Her eyes almost popped out of her head. "I won?"

"You won," said Larry with a grin. "They

want you up there." He motioned toward the stand where Mr. Smelker stood at the mike.

Suddenly Teddy Jo's heart leaped and she almost ran to receive her blue ribbon.

13
The Noise in the Shed

Monday after school Teddy Jo ran beside Paul
into Grandpa's backyard. She pulled off her
jacket and tied the sleeves around her waist.
It was warm once again without a sign of snow.
The deer hunters wouldn't be very happy, but
Dad wouldn't care. He and Mom had gone out
early Saturday morning and each got a deer,
Dad a six-point and Mom a four-point. Their
freezer would soon be full of venison and that
made Dad happy. Sunday afternoon he'd sat
with the family and talked about hunting. He'd
said that he liked the fresh air and complete
silence around him in the woods. Factory work
rang constantly in his ears and he needed the
silence and peacefulness of the woods. Mom
had said having venison in the freezer cut down
the grocery bill.

Smokey nickered and ran to the gate. Paul
tossed a handful of hay over to him. "I'll get

you water now, Smokey." Paul had waited impatiently all day in school to come see Smokey, Queen, and the remaining puppy.

"I hope Grandpa didn't find a home for the puppy yet," said Teddy Jo. She looked toward the kennel, then frowned. "Paul? Paul, I don't see Queen!"

"She might be in the doghouse."

"But she's been coming to the gate to us and she didn't this time." Teddy Jo ran to the kennel. "Queen! Here, Queenie."

There was no sign of the big gold collie.

Paul flung wide the gate. "Queenie! Queenie!" He ducked down and looked in the doghouse. It was empty, and his heart fell to his feet. Would Grandpa give Queen away without telling them?

"Her leash is gone," said Teddy Jo in a strangled voice as she touched the hook to the side of the doghouse. "I know Grandpa wouldn't give her away unless he talked to us first. He told us every time he found a home for one of the puppies." She clapped her hand to her mouth. "The puppy! What if it's gone too?"

The puppy *was* gone too and Teddy Jo blinked back tears. Paul shook his head and leaned weakly against the shed.

"What're we going to do?" asked Paul lifelessly.

"I don't know, Paulie."

Just then Anna walked around the garage to

the back door. She stopped when she saw them. "Hi, kids. Is anything wrong?"

Paul ran to her, shouting that Queen and the puppy were gone. Teddy Jo hung back, waiting for Anna to say something that would suddenly make everything right.

"I've been at the library all afternoon, so I don't know where they went. I hope they didn't get out and run away." Her forehead wrinkled in concern as she looked toward the empty kennel. "I don't know what your grandpa will say about this. He cares as much for Queen as you children do."

"We'll go look for her," said Paul. "Right, Teddy Jo?"

She nodded, suddenly frightened for Queen and the puppy. If they were running in the woods now, they could easily be shot by a hunter. Her stomach tightened and she almost moaned aloud.

Anna told them good-bye and walked inside. Smokey nickered again. A blue jay scolded from the tree where the tire swing hung.

Teddy Jo gripped Paul's arm and he looked up at her in alarm. "I think Roger Peck came here and took Queen or set her free. Let's go find Roger and maybe we'll find Queen and her puppy."

"I'm going to punch him right in the nose when I find him." Paul doubled his fists and danced around, jabbing and thrusting.

"We can't take the shortcut because of

hunters." She shook her head impatiently and her dark hair bounced. "We'll have to stay on the road. Let's go!"

Much later Teddy Jo stopped at Peck's driveway, her chest heaving and her face red. "We'll have to be very quiet, Paul. Very quiet."

"Their pickup is gone." Shivers of fear ran over Paul and he suddenly had to go to the bathroom. He sure couldn't take the time now. He'd have to make himself wait until they got back to Grandpa's.

Slowly Teddy Jo crept along the drive with Paul behind her. She could hear his ragged breathing and she knew the run had tired him out. Her legs felt weak and rubbery. She stopped outside the shed, her head cocked, listening for any sound. Something or someone was moving around inside. Was it Queen and the pup? Or were Roger and his dad inside?

Suddenly the door swung open and Roger stepped out. His face turned white when he saw them and he jerked the door shut with a bang. "What're you two spying around here for? Get home where you belong!"

"Where's Queen?" asked Paul, stepping forward with his fists doubled. His voice didn't quiver at all and he asked again, "Where is our dog and her pup?"

"We want her back," said Teddy Jo sharply.

"I hope you never get her back and then we'll be even because of Smokey. Now, get away from here and leave me alone!"

Teddy Jo glanced over Roger's shoulder at the shed. Something was in there that Roger didn't want them to see. It had to be Queen. She took a step toward it and Roger pushed her back.

"Don't go near that shed unless you want your head busted!" Roger's tattered jacket hung open. A stain darkened his shirt and jeans.

"You can't stop me, Roger Peck!" cried Teddy Jo as she lunged for the closed shed door.

Roger's arm shot out and he blocked her way, knocking the air from her. She gasped and stumbled back against Paul. He dodged around her and rammed his head into Roger's stomach. Roger slumped to the ground, holding his stomach and groaning. Paul gasped and stared down at the high school boy. Wow! He'd really done it! He wasn't such a chicken after all.

Teddy Jo fumbled with the catch and finally pushed the shed door open.

"Don't!" croaked Roger, struggling to his feet. "I'll get it from my dad if you look in there."

Teddy Jo looked inside, then covered her mouth with her hand. Three gutted deer hung from the rafters and none of them had tags on them.

"I hope you're satisfied," snapped Roger.

"I don't have your dumb dog and I never did have."

"Then where is she?" asked Paul, looking all around. All he saw was a pile of rubbish in the weedy yard. Trees surrounded the property. Was Queen somewhere running loose where a hunter could shoot her? His eyes stung with tears and he wanted to ram into Roger again just to bring back the exciting feeling.

Teddy Jo swallowed hard. "Did your dad shoot those doe?"

Roger latched the door shut. "Yeah. Are you going to tell?"

Teddy Jo's eyes flashed. "Yes! Yes, I'm going to tell everybody that will listen! Do you know how terrible it is to shoot deer, and without a special license? Sure, I'll tell!"

Roger caught her arm and his fingers bit into her arm. "Don't do it, Teddy Jo. Please."

She saw his panic and she stood very still.

"Dad'll beat me if he knows anyone saw in the shed. He told me to guard it. He'll have the deer out of here tonight and then we're leaving. This time he said we're going to Detroit. He said he'd let this place go for back taxes."

Teddy Jo tugged and Roger released her. "I won't tell, Roger. I should, but I don't want you to get in trouble. Just tell me what you did with Queen."

"I didn't do anything with her. I didn't go

to Ed Korman's place. I wouldn't dare."

Paul sagged against the side of the shed. Where was Queen? Where was the pup? Maybe Grandpa had given them both away without first telling them.

"You two get out of here before my dad gets back or he'll make real trouble for you," said Roger in a rush as he looked toward the road.

Teddy Jo caught Paul's arm and pulled him along with her. She looked back over her shoulder at Roger. "Does Linda know that you're leaving again?"

"I'm going to call her later. Don't tell her what my dad did, will you? I don't want her to know." Roger stood with his hands stuffed in his ragged jacket pockets and his feet apart. He looked unhappy and Teddy Jo felt sorry for him.

"We won't tell Linda. Me and Paul won't tell anything." She turned away and walked to the dirt road with Paul.

Paul was quiet a long time. The sun warmed his head. He stopped and cupped his hands around his mouth. "Queen! Queenie, come here!"

Teddy Jo kept walking, her throat tight. She would not cry. She was no baby. A tear slipped out and splashed to the dust at her feet.

14
A Happy Day

Paul dashed through Grandpa's kitchen to the
bathroom, slamming the door behind him.

"A hurricane," said Anna with a soft laugh.

Teddy Jo's chin quivered and she looked
down at the floor. The room smelled like fresh
coffee and spicy chili.

"What's wrong, Teddy Jo?" Anna's warm
voice wrapped around Teddy Jo's heart.
"Didn't you find any sign of the dog?"

"No." Her vision blurred with tears.

"I'm so sorry. I know how much I love
Honey and I know that you love your dog as
much." Anna touched Teddy Jo's arm.

The wall that she'd erected suddenly melted
and Teddy Jo turned into Anna's arms for her
comfort and love. Anna smelled good and felt
soft and warm. Finally Teddy Jo lifted her
head and smiled. Anna kissed her cheeks, then
smiled.

"Thanks, Teddy Jo."

"Thanks?"

"I'm thankful that you've finally let me past that barrier. You're very important to me and I wanted you to feel the same about me." Anna sat on an oak kitchen chair and Teddy Jo sat beside her in the chair where Grandpa always sat. A bouquet of orange and yellow chrysanthemums stood in a white vase in the middle of the table. "I never wanted to take your grandpa away from you, and I think you know that."

Teddy Jo grinned and pushed her hands under her legs. "I know. He still loves me just as much as before. He's my grandpa."

"And now I'm your grandma. When you're comfortable with that, would you call me Grandma?"

Teddy Jo thought about that and rolled the name over on her tongue, then finally nodded.

"I can call you Grandma, too," said Paul from the doorway. "Is that all right?" His shirt was half in and half out of his baggy jeans. His shoelaces dragged on the floor and he was grinning as if he were proud of himself.

"Of course you can, Paul," said Anna. "But right now it's time for you both to get home before your parents worry about you."

Later Teddy Jo walked into the kitchen at home and smelled the ham that was planned for supper. Carol turned from the refrigerator with a head of lettuce in her hand.

"I asked Grandpa and Anna to come for

supper and he said they'd be here about six. You kids wash up and change out of those clothes. It looks like you've been playing in the dirt."

"I didn't know Grandpa was coming for supper," said Teddy Jo. "We just talked to . . . to Grandma and she didn't say anything."

Paul stepped forward. "Grandma didn't say anything." It felt great to say *grandma*. Inside his head he said it over and over. Grandma, grandma, grandma. He ran to the bathroom to wash and looked in the mirror and said it again.

Inside her bedroom Teddy Jo changed into clean jeans and a long-sleeved tee shirt. As she brushed her hair, the door opened and Linda walked in. Her eyes and nose were red from crying and she twisted a strand of hair around her finger.

"Roger's leaving tonight and I might never see him again. I don't know if I can survive!"

"Oh, Linda, I'm sorry." Teddy Jo set the hairbrush on the dresser. "Maybe he'll write to you."

"Maybe. He said he saw you. Did he look all right? Was he happy about leaving?"

"I know he likes you a lot, Linda. I don't think he wanted to leave you, but he had to go with his dad. Maybe he'll be happy in Detroit."

"Maybe." Linda wiped a tear off her cheek. "I hope so! I don't want anything bad to happen to him!"

Teddy Jo swallowed hard. "Linda, I'll pray for him if you want. God does answer prayer."

Linda chewed her bottom lip, then nodded. "Do pray for him. I wish I could. Maybe someday. Maybe." She rushed from the room, leaving a trail of perfume.

At supper Linda picked at her food. Teddy Jo was too hungry to let her concern over the missing dog stop her appetite. She listened to Grandpa and Grandma talk to Mom and Dad. Dad and Grandpa both seemed extra excited.

Finally Teddy Jo finished her strawberry Jell-O with banana slices. She looked up to find Grandpa watching her, a twinkle in his eye. "What?" she asked just above a whisper.

"I have a surprise for you outdoors."

"This is the time to check it out," said Larry with a grin. He scraped back his chair. "Ed and I can't keep this to ourselves another minute."

"Come outdoors," said Grandpa, swinging the back door wide.

"What is this?" asked Anna as she stood.

Teddy Jo walked with Paul behind Dad. Her stomach fluttered with excitement. Something was up and she couldn't wait to learn what it was. Suddenly she stopped and stared. Right at the corner of the house stood a small dog-house. She lifted startled eyes to Grandpa, then Dad.

Paul dropped to his knees and peeked inside the doghouse, then carefully pulled on the chain. The missing puppy tumbled out and Paul cuddled him close.

"He was missing," said Teddy Jo, shaking her head.

"I took him to the vet for shots and a tag," said Grandpa. "Your dad said that you kids could have the last puppy."

"Oh, my," said Teddy Jo.

"Me, too?" asked Linda just above a whisper.

"You, too," said Larry, nodding.

Linda slowly sank to the soft grass and touched a furry spot on the puppy that Teddy Jo and Paul weren't petting.

Finally Teddy Jo looked up, tears sparkling in her eyes. "Thanks, Dad. We thought some-one stole Queen and the puppy."

Dad shook his head and Grandpa knelt beside Teddy Jo.

"I took Queen to the vet's for shots and a tag, too. I've decided to keep Queen for myself. We get along and I just couldn't part with her."

"I'm glad," whispered Teddy Jo. She turned her eyes back on Dad. "I never thought you'd want us to have a dog."

"You have changed, Larry," said Carol.

Larry shrugged and cleared his throat. A gentle wind blew his hair. He stuffed his hands into his jeans pockets. "I've been waiting for just the right time to tell everyone. I guess this is as good a time as any." He cleared his throat and looked right into Carol's eyes. "Two months ago I decided I wanted my life changed. I saw the change in Teddy Jo and Paul and then in you. I knew Jesus made the difference. I knew that I wanted to be a new creation the way you showed me in the Bible. I'm a Christian. I was a little scared to tell you before."

"Oh, Larry!" Carol wrapped her arms around him and sobbed softly against his shoulder.

Teddy Jo sat cross-legged on the grass and looked at Mom and Dad. Grandpa had been right. They were a Christian family. Only Linda was left and she'd said maybe someday.

The puppy licked her hand and she giggled.

"Let's give him a perfect name," said Paul.

"But we've been trying to think of a name for a long time, and couldn't," said Teddy Jo.

Linda pushed her fingers into the puppy's long fur. "I have a name, a perfect name."

"What?" Teddy Jo and Paul asked at once.

Linda smiled. "Happy. We'll call him Happy. He makes us happy and he is happy."

"Happy," said Teddy Jo with a nod. She looked at Grandpa and he nodded and winked. "Happy. That's the best name ever."